About

Exit the Jingle Man

Menalcus Lankford's *Exit the Jingle Man* addresses serious topics without losing a sense of humor. His engaging narrative style allows him to cover stresses in family relations, the positive and negative aspects of growing old, and the challenges of life in general, while emphasizing the quirks and charms of his unusual characters.

~~ Anne Wyatt Brown, emeritus associate professor at the University of Florida and former co-editor of the *Journal of Aging, Humanities, and the Arts*. She is the author of *Barbara Pym: A Critical Biography,* a study of the English novelist.

Menalcus Lankford has written an engaging book in which each character has an edge and an eccentricity. Their adventures embody the influences and connections, both known and unknown, in all our lives. Lankford's prose skillfully combines humor with pathos. I not only enjoyed the stories but found myself reflecting upon the characters long after I had finished reading."

~~ Edwin Lynn, author of *Shore Lines* and *Tired Dragons.*

Exit the Jingle Man

What we live, what we leave behind

Menalcus Lankford

Chapter one: "Journey into Spring" was published in a slightly different form in the January-March 2010 issue of the *Journal of Aging, Humanities and the Arts,* the official journal of the Gerontological Society of America, a publication of the Taylor & Francis Group of Routledge.

Contents

Chapter One:
Journey into Spring

At age 90 Ted was in the hospital for tests and observation, but that wasn't what he was worried about. He looked across at Buff, who shared his semi-private room, and decided the worry had grown big enough to interrupt the man's reading. "Hey, excuse me, but please tell me your opinion on nursing homes."

The man put down the newspaper baseball pages Ted had lent him. "I wouldn't know," he said. "Seems there's all grades. High-toned places where it's fancy dining room and vans that take you to the symphony, and cheap ones where you're stuck in a clinic looking place, surrounded by hacking, drooling, whining old folks. Bad show. Why you ask?"

"My niece wants to plant me in one. Starting tomorrow, when she takes me out of here. Afraid I'm scheduled for the B movie type you describe, as I don't have enough money for the A movie."

Buff made a short sound of sympathy, looked embarrassed and hid his face back in the newspaper. "Well, good luck on that."

But Ted couldn't let it go. "To move into such a place, you'd have to be satisfied with your life — right?"

"Meaning?"

"The life you had lived up till then. Because you sure couldn't do much about it once you're stuck there. Half the inmates out of their heads and messing their pants, and the poor orderlies and nurses having to put up with it all." Ted sighed and pressed on. "And people dying around me every week. I wouldn't appreciate that. I wouldn't do it myself."

"You wouldn't die around yourself?"

"I wouldn't think of doing such a thing."

Buff put down the paper. "Tell me, Mr. Theodore. What you said about needing to be satisfied with your life before going into a nursing home — just what is it you still want to do at age ninety? More advertising jingles?"

"Not that! Write more pitches so folks will go buy more junk – I got sick of doing those long ago."

"I don't know about that. You've rattled off a bunch of them in here."

"They're still stuck in my head is all. They drop in uninvited. Feel like I wasted my life, making up all those lies."

Buff looked troubled. "'Wasted your life on lies'? That's tough stuff."

"Lady Fortune looks away,
Leaving you in deep despair?
Come back at her another day,
With a dab of Bryl Creem in your hair!"

"Jeez, that one *is* pretty bad."

"You see — it just dropped into my head. Like that "little dab" is the answer to my prayer. The solution on the nursing home."

"I don't remember that one."

"The company didn't buy it. Doesn't mean I can forget it."

There was the noise of a family in the corridor. Ted's favorite thing about the hospital, this added a little life, and you could try to imagine the people who were saying those things and what they meant. Now it sounded like a mother and father arguing about a relative's hospital bill, and their kid trying to get in a word edgewise. Something about getting taken to an Orioles game.

"But you did other stuff besides jingles," Buff was saying. "Yesterday you mentioned volunteering in a inner city school. That was a good thing."

"Yeah. I'd done that for twenty years, but in December I had to quit."

"Oh? How come?"

"For years it worked — me coaching the slow learners in reading and writing. Did I tell you that I would make up jiving rhymes and get them to do the same, then write them down? That was one thing I got from all those years as jingle man — I could make up stuff. But now the kids won't pay attention, so I can't do it. They haven't learned respect in the home."

"That's a shame. A bloody shame."

"The only thing they respect is money and flash."

Buff looked sad for him. Ted thought he didn't have good color in his face, and wondered if that was due to the kidney problem he was here for.

"As for the money, I don't have much," he told the man. "And when you're ninety, it's hard to impress a thirteen year old with your flash."

"Don't sell yourself short. I find on a good day it's still possible to show off a little sparkle."

"Maybe for you, at eighty-one. You're still a wild and crazy kid."

Buff was saying something, but Ted had gone back to listening to the conversation in the hall — parents and their boy. Sounded like they were telling him to wait there, while they went off to argue with the hospital.

"Did you say it's tomorrow morning that niece of yours is taking you out of here?"

"Hey, buddy!" Ted had shouted in the loudest voice he could manage into the hall beyond. "You an Oriole fan?"

After a moment, that brought the boy. A shy face, looking in at them from the door. He might be thirteen.

"So you think they're going to do any better this season?"

Now the face was starting to brighten. "Yeah — they got that new catcher who's going to be a star. And Ray is coming back, and they signed up Brian, and Adam Jones might be a star too." The boy had taken one step into the room. He was watching Buff to see whether he had any objection.

"Come in, son," Buff said. "We're all baseball fans here. Tell us what you think."

Another step into the room. "I think the whole team is more excited to win," the boy said. "But I know the starting pitchers might be bad."

Ted nodded. "True. Not much experience there. But being excited to win does make a difference." He took a moment to drink in the light in the boy's face. At that age, he'd been just as thrilled about the then minor league Orioles. He had been a shy kid too, but not when he got to a game. With complete strangers he would talk baseball, becoming a different person.

He looked back at the boy. "Did I hear you asking your folks to take you to a game?"

Shadow crossing the face, still beardless. "Yeah, but they're not so sure. It costs a lot… And my dad's not a fan."

"Well, look!" Ted burst out. "You got a birthday coming up?"

"June tenth."

"Well, look. Tell them that's what you want. That can be your present! How old will you be?"

"Thirteen."

"So tell them this is a very big birthday for you — the start of being a teenager, for heaven's sake. And that's the only present you want. Tell them it doesn't have to be expensive seats. You just want to be there — right?"

"That's it. I just want to be there."

Buff started talking to the boy about the pitching situation, but then there was a noise outside, and suddenly the parents were there — he in a sweatshirt and jeans and she wearing a tight little stiff-shouldered suit and a u-shaped hat of yellow fibers that looked like an abandoned bird's nest.

They were staring into the room, seemingly shocked that their shy son had ventured in to talk to two strangers. They called him abruptly away, without even a nod. What did they care about two old codgers wired up in beds? They vanished as quickly as possible into their own lives.

"It's spring training time," Buff said. "Everyone gets excited for the season ahead. Whether you're twelve, eighty or ninety, it's a time to dream."

"Exactly." Ted paused, waiting for some new association to swim complete into his brain. "You just reminded me of a true story that I like very much. You game?"

"Sure. It's not like I have a busy social calendar in here."

"Oh, it's just short anyway. Two friends work for the same big company, and both are sick of the office in-fighting and general tiresome of the place. It's early February, and they feel stuck also in endless dreary winter, every day cold and gray. One goes and sticks a folded-over note in the mailbox of the other. Amidst the discouragement of work and winter, the other goes to his mailbox that day and pulls out the note. It says simply: "Cheer up — next week pitchers and catchers report."

Buff was nodding, duly impressed.

"I always found that a very sweet story."

"Yep. Gotta have faith. Spring will come."

"Of course, it's already come down in Florida, where they're practicing for the season in seventy, eighty degree weather."

Buff began to talk in detail about the season ahead, but Ted had stopped listening. Now he interrupted the man: "Fort Lauderdale, where the Orioles are for spring training — that's on the rail line, is it?"

"Wouldn't know. When my wife and I used to go down to take in a few games, we would fly."

Ted was gazing out the window at the brick wall beyond the dead little tree in the courtyard. "You know, it's really awful to me that I can't work with those school kids anymore."

Buff nodded, looked away.

"Do you happen to know what time the hospital signs out patients in the morning? Because it's tomorrow she comes for me, you understand."

"Might be ten o'clock. You said it's your niece will pick you up?"

"Well, she's the widow of my nephew. His mom, my sister, has died too, leaving her the one who is planning to take me away to the B movie nursing home. What they call it reminds me of the kind of lying jingles I used to write — 'Shangri La Senior Spa'."

2

"He's *what!*" Robyn stood straight and shoved the cell phone tight against her ear. Her voice had broken so shrill that the old black cat recoiled in the corner, drew up its back and briefly bared its teeth.

"How can that happen? Johns Hopkins, supposedly the best hospital in the world, simply loses a patient?

An old man wired up in bed, monitored by the nurses' station, and suddenly you can't find him. How's that possible?"

And now here came her mousy apartment mate, Miss Mildred, drawn by the hullabaloo. As usual creeping into the room like something might break. "You absolutely sure he's not in any of the buildings? ... Did you call the police? Well, thanks at least for that." She paused to listen, then broke in again: "I got another call. It could be the police. I'll be back at you — don't worry about that!

"Yes, officer — still has a car he hardly drives. Right, parked at his apartment. ... Absolutely my permission to search, but I doubt you'll get any help there." A moment later she thanked the officer and turned to Mildred.

"Can you believe it? That goofy Uncle Ted has gone missing from the hospital. Sometime after five-fifteen in the morning. That's when the police found his heart monitor was interrupted."

"My goodness. Did he just walk out?"

"Seems so. The police can't find that he phoned a cab."

"Isn't he too ill for that? Didn't you say he was in there for heart attacks?"

Robyn shook her head disgustedly. "Maybe, maybe not. The doctor said, 'Some type of cardiovascular events.' But he's been passing out at odd times. People from his church and apartment building call me about that. And it's just not my job to keep checking on him!"

"So did you say you're putting him in a nursing home?"

"Yeah, I found one that's a deal. See, he pays a lot of rent — too big an apartment now that he's by himself, but I couldn't get him to move to a cheaper place because he lived there so long with his wife. But subtracting that rent, selling his car, getting rid of that insurance, etc. – with those savings he can afford this place."

"Be a big change from being on his own. How you think he'll do?"

Robyn shrugged, annoyed. "You can't figure with an old man like that. He knows its risky to live on his own, but then I suggest a practical solution, and he's like a rebellious teenager."

"Well, it's awful he might be wandering the streets in that neighborhood around the hospital."

"Maybe not," Robyn said. "He's just an old man, wife dead, no children. No good anymore to himself, or anyone else really. Going this way — there could be worse things."

"Than being mugged out there, maybe left dying in the street?"

"At least then it's over quick. There can be worse things."

Robyn let the mousy one ponder that, while she herself stooped and fondled the top of the old cat's head. "Poor little Gretchy — did Moma's yelling on the phone scare you? Sowwy, you poor old thing." The cat purred and arched its back against the caressing hand.

"Won't you be late to work?" she asked Mildred.

"You're right – it's time. But I don't blame you for being upset at the hospital."

"It's a clear case of negligence. Someone at the nursing station likely fell asleep. His heart monitor was off for forty minutes before anyone noticed, even though a red light starts flashing — I have that from the police. That's evidence in a court."

"I'd be really mad at them myself."

Robyn gave her a slight smile. "I can't afford not to be. You know, don't you, that they're a multi-billion dollar corporation with a big reputation to protect?"

What she wouldn't tell her was the other piece: that the hefty beginning payment to that cheesy nursing home — including the deposit and three months advance rent — was to have been paid when they arrived at the place today, and maybe now that cash could stay in the old man's accounts. And from there it would all go by the will directly to her daughter Joanie, a minor — his last surviving kin by blood.

<u>3</u>

With his pajamas and toiletries inside the shoulder bag he had brought to the hospital, he peeked into the dim hall. No one. This time of morning, peaceful as a morgue. Only sound — Buff innocently snoring away behind him in the room.

He would have liked to walk out through the original building past the twelve foot high Christ, at whose feet folks would leave touching notes asking for help. Could use some of that himself for this adventure. But he might be spotted trying to pick his way through the maze of hospital halls — better take the quickest way to the outside.

One thing was clear: there could be no taxicabs. One of the first things the police checked in a case like this, at least according to the crime shows: "To all drivers: anyone do a pick up near Hopkins Hospital of a thin, old, white-haired, white man between five-fifteen and six-fifteen this morning? Carrying a brown cloth shoulder bag."

So lucky a subway station was right in front. Exiting through the side street door, he felt the cold air hit him, but once he turned the corner there it was: a cozy warm retreat in the Broadway median. The trains started running at five, so he would be out of here like nothing. And no one would remember an old man on the subway.

It didn't take the train long. "State Center" — the closest stop to Penn Station, and he was there at 5:53. Only a few blocks to walk, but it was colder than he'd realized. He should be wearing more than this sport jacket. The wind in his face made it hard to walk, and now came this tightness of breath that off and on would afflict him these days.

Last night lying in the hospital bed, he'd figured out how to do the trains. He wouldn't hang around the Baltimore station waiting for the long distance train he wanted. Too risky — police would be on the lookout for him. First he'd grab one of the frequent commuter locals down to Washington. Safely out of Baltimore, he would wait for the Silver Star in the big beautiful station there, where no one would be watching for him. When it arrived around noon, he would have a private room in a sleeping car, so in case his picture hit television he would be mostly out of sight — not to mention that he was too old to spend the night sitting up in a day coach. The sleeper would cost a lot, more than he could normally afford, but he didn't expect to be needing money much longer.

This excitement had started just yesterday afternoon from talking nursing homes with Buff, and how there was still something needed in his life, especially now that he couldn't any longer help the school kids. Something he couldn't satisfy in any nursing home. And then talking baseball with that boy. Seeing the light in his face and remembering.

The station loomed ahead, fronted now by that stupid monstrosity of a statue, a silver hermaphrodite cut-out. Just in time — out of breath in this wind.

In the waiting room he had a brainstorm: buy his cheap Senior Ticket at one of the machines, so there would be no agent to remember him. He had trouble at first, but a young man kindly stepped forward to help him figure it out, and then it popped out of the machine like magic — like a ticket to a new life.

With a few minutes to wait, he plopped down on a bench. For a moment he leaned his head back to catch his breath, staring up at the handsome stained glass skylight. He wished he could give that hospital boy and his dad good tickets to a game. But no way of finding them now. More troubling was that being pushed into the hospital by his dead nephew's wife Robyn — to be followed immediately by the nursing home — he may not have made it clear enough what he wished to leave to her teenage daughter Joan, his best friend in the world now.

When the train came in, he lucked out in the crowd of boarding commuters and got a window seat at the second level. From up here you could watch the world glide by below and feel the wonder in that.

As soon as the train pulled out, he felt that he was escaping. Only around Baltimore would the police be looking for him.

Once out of the city, it was so hopeful gazing out at the low-angled sun glinting off frosty fields, as though the beginning of this day was connected to all beginnings rising forever over that horizon.

In this mood he began to make allowances for Robyn. So much easier to do now that he was beyond her clutches. She was just not a person who had patience — that was all. So no surprise she didn't have time for the fainting spells and medical tests of an old man who was no more to her than the uncle of her dead husband. And he was convinced that she had never much loved his nephew, which made it the more understandable. True, she was awful cheap with money, but she had grown up poor, so she was just scared that way. Just clutching tight, as people would. The way she saw it, the nursing home was the place that would take care of him and get him out of her life. The way *he* saw it, after discussing it with Buff and thinking more about it, the nursing home was the place that would limit his body and cramp his soul, leaving him hardly any space to breathe.

And she had the goods on him. From the fainting spells and various tests, she had got a head doctor in the hospital to sign something saying that Mr.

Theodore Costas could no longer live safely on his own because of medical considerations. She had told him that — maybe her big mistake!

In Washington Union Station, he went into a restaurant and ordered a big breakfast. Hadn't done that in years. Of course, no one had any appetite in a hospital, but it was longer than that since he'd eaten a big meal. This whole idea — which was still taking shape — seemed to be taking years off his life. For the moment.

After breakfast he stood in line for a ticket agent. With joy in his voice, he told the man, "I want a bedroom to Fort Lauderdale on the Star."

He was an older Black man, very dignified and with a moustache turned white. Efficient too — didn't take him long to find the space available on his computer. "Did you want roundtrip in a sleeper, and to reserve your return room?"

"No sir. I'm just going one way."

Maybe it was something in the way he said it, because the agent looked at him with a question mark in his eyes. His dark brows were also turning white, and the eyes had depths to them.

When told the cost, he didn't even swallow, because this was a once in a lifetime.

"How would you like to pay for this, sir?"

"Credit card. Don't have my checkbook." He handed it over, and just at the point that the man was about to swipe it, he cried out — not even knowing why yet: "Wait! Stop!"

It came out loud, and the agent gave a little jump.

"Sorry. I just realized something and didn't want you to swipe the card."

What he had realized is that he might be traced through the charge. If they knew his credit card number, the police would be watching the account as a clue to his whereabouts. All they would need to see is the charge for a ticket on the Silver Star to Fort Lauderdale, and they would have him. Game over. Back home and into that nursing home. Do not pass go.

"Sir, what do you want me to do?"

He shook his head. "I got to think. Likely I'll come back later. Thank you, and I do apologize for acting like a crazy man."

He sank into a bucket seat in the waiting area, and stared at the ceiling. *The question is what can Robyn tell the police about my credit card?*

He had told her about some false charges on it around Christmas, so she would know he had one. She wouldn't know the number, but if she had ever seen him pull it out, she might have noticed the issuing bank. And with that information, the police could probably look up the number. No one at church – no one else living would know. Mike might have known, from when they would go out each week for bar food, but he had passed in January, bless his soul. But had Robyn ever seen the card and maybe the bank behind it? He just couldn't remember.

So now he was anxious again, drat it! Just what you didn't need, what you ought to be able to leave behind at ninety years old, for heaven's sake. What this trip was supposed to be all about — not worrying his mind but following his best deep instinct down to a spring training place he had never been except in the dreams of his youth and the longings of his heart.

He didn't know how long he sat there trying to remember about Robyn and his credit card, but suddenly that ticket agent was standing before him, saying in a gentle voice, "Sir, I wanted you to know we got only one bedroom left on that train. So if you want it..."

That decided him. The spirit in which the man said this – when that spirit came to you, there was nothing but to let yourself be swept up in it and not worry over details. He would charge the ticket on his card and trust to Providence. "Thank you, sir. I do appreciate that. You have gone beyond the call of duty, and that is rare and a blessing in this life."

So promising here, he was thinking at half past noon from the easy chair in his bedroom as the long silver train rolled onto the bridge, south bound over the Potomac. Outside the big window it was snowing hard, but he was comfortable, warming his left foot on the low radiator. Because of the credit card charge, he knew it all might end at any moment. What was that old movie with Cary Grant on the run and hiding in this blonde's compartment, when the police stopped and searched the train? He didn't have any blonde to close him up in her upper berth if the police knocked. But every moment this lasted was the chance of a lifetime.

The snow had covered the ground, and he was starting to doze, when he saw something that really woke him up. It looked just the same — first the college to the left of the tracks, then the station and the main street of the small town. He hadn't thought of this in decades, though his moments there had been so striking.

It had been a Sunday afternoon when he was a college student, and he was waiting at this same station — by which this present train was passing now at reduced speed but not stopping — when he had seen that girl. She had been walking along the platform with her boyfriend, having just gotten off the train from New York, where they had been for the weekend. He had been waiting for the train from the other direction to take him back to U. Pennsylvania, having been down visiting friends at this Virginia college.

The girl had run with a different crowd in Baltimore, and his memories of her were unpleasant.

She had been in a group from a different school – they had teased him and his pals at a dance. Snide and superior, they had seemed.

There had been an awkward moment when neither he nor this girl he barely knew seemed sure of whether to acknowledge the other. But then they had, and only a couple of years after high school everything had changed. Maybe it was just the surprise of running into each other and getting a breath of home in the midst of being away at college — whatever it was, they had stood and talked on the platform, her boyfriend waiting patiently beside her. Talked about the hometown, their schools, the people they knew and — the important part — about how high school students got too taken up with back-biting and cliques, and how silly they both had been.

"So you're saying I was actually no more dumb-acting than most," he remembered asking her.

Now, seventy years later, he could still hear the warmth in her responding voice: "Oh, no. And all us girls actually respected you. We knew you were a boy to be trusted."

That had affected him more than he had allowed to show. But his train had come in just then, and he waved goodbye and climbed on board, headed back to his college life in Philadelphia.

He had found a window seat in the coach, casually glanced out and been surprised to see her waving vigorously at him in a sort of parody of enthusiasm, but with a big, good-hearted grin as she stood beside her stoic boyfriend. Waving back, he had kept looking at her — because the whole thing was so much fun, so delightful — until the train pulled out.

That had turned out to be the parting wave in their lives. They had never seen each other since that afternoon.

He breathed deep and sat back in the armchair. Somehow he had turned into the old man that he was now. Would she also be alive at ninety?

That little town had been Ashland, maybe thirty miles north of Richmond. And the college he had visited that weekend in maybe…1938 was Randolph Macon. Still there — he had recognized it in passing.

"A boy to be trusted." At the time that had felt good to hear. In the twenty years following that long ago Sunday afternoon, he'd had a checkered career — done things he was not proud of. So had she been right: "a boy to be trusted"? Maybe at some basic level yes, but with all his bragging and sneaky maneuvering for advantage — well, it was hard to make a final judgment on that. He had never done anything criminal, and in later years he had reformed a bit, but in the quest to claw his way ahead and sell others on the value of his little talking self he had done a fair amount of tearing up precious things with those claws — a fair amount of ripping and tearing.

If you rip it,
If you tear it,
Solomon Parrot,
Will repair it!

"Oh, shut up!" he cried aloud in the little train room. "Death to you and all of the jingles – get out of my brain!

Maybe he could just hand over to Solomon Parrot, Cleaners and Menders, his whole life to repair, freeing him of regrets.

Too late for that: the man, twenty years his senior, would be long dead. But maybe he had passed the firm on to children and grandchildren. Maybe even to this day there would be lots of little Parrots squawking around, repairing everything they could get their little claws on.

On that note, he realized how tired he was, having slept little and risen at five to dress and sneak out of the hospital. He wrapped himself in an extra blanket he found in the small clothes closet, pulled down the window shade against the swirling snow and began to murmur over and over a simple prayer to drive all the absurd, life-fixing jingles from his brain. By degrees it worked, and he slept.

He slept a long time, and when he awoke and pushed up the shade, the snow was gone. The porter soon knocked on the door and took his dinner reservation.

"Where are we?" he asked the man.

"Oh, now we almost to South Carolina."

Renewed energy now for this adventure – on with the shoes, the sport jacket and off to the lounge car!

He took the last open armchair, sitting among facing rows of fellow seniors. Lots of white heads toasting the on-rushing approach of warmer lands. For this moment pleasantly flushed with booze and anticipation of what lay ahead of them. But not too far ahead.

In the dining car he was pleased when the steward seated no white heads at his table but a young couple, facing him. Their greeting was friendly enough, but they seemed nervously distracted, and now he guessed why: the prices on the menu.

In an instant he knew what he would do — it was only finding a good way.

Turned out they were bound for Savannah, which he remembered so pleasantly for its Spanish moss draped formal squares, and when he found what he'd suspected — that they were college students — he knew he had it. "Oh, what school?" "N.C. State in Raleigh. We're just going home for Spring Break." "College students like to move around, don't they? Even in my time that was popular. I would go from the University of Pennsylvania to New York City for the weekend, or home to Baltimore. Once I went to Ashland, Virginia — to visit friends at Randolph Macon College." "Yeah, we like to do that. But it can get expensive." "Right, well look — since you're college students, if you'd let me interview you over dinner, I could put you on my expense account and pay for everything. You see, I'm doing a project studying college student life today. Your names of course would not be used."

It was so good to see their young faces lighten at that. And these were very forthright kids, sharing their worries, their doubts about things. He took notes all over the ticket envelope from his jacket pocket to make it look good, and though he had little wise advise to offer, he kept hearing in his head not a stupid jingle answer for once but something a saint was known for saying: *All will be well, and all will be well and all manner of things will be well.* He tried to convey that to them in his manner of reassurance.

Toward the end they made a half-joking reference to a tension between them over their pace of response to things that needed to be dealt with, and he could honestly tell them that he'd had the same problem with his wife. "We all move at different speeds, but we do all move on. When she died at eighty-five, I lost the true companion of my life."

When the check came, he put it on that same credit card, which could be his undoing at any moment but hadn't been yet. He was saving cash for a quite large tip to the porter.

After the two of them left the table, he realized that he had been so moved by the boy's speaking of the death last year of his father that there was something he must tell him from his own youth. He put it into a short note — that seemed the best way, given how personal it was — and managed to slip it unnoticed into the open side pocket of the boy's bag as he passed them on the way back to his sleeper room. His own father gone so early – had his whole life been a search for some replacement?

Back in his room, he doused the light, watched the moonlit scene roll by outside the window and began to replay his life with Estelle.

By eleven o'clock he was snug in bed. Pulling it down, the porter had told him they were almost to Savannah, and he drowsily imagined the young college couple stepping onto the platform, being met by parents and telling excitedly about meeting an old man on the train who, once they agreed to participate in his survey, had paid for their dinner on his expense account.

Up at four a.m., wide-awake, and he knew why: the long nap in the afternoon, plus being an early riser anyway. No more sleep possible now, and everything dark in the world fleeing by his window, so he would dress and walk around.

The corridors of the sleeping cars were as silent as that hospital hall he had stepped into at five-something this morning. But there might be some action in the cars ahead.

The diner and lounge cars were dimly lit and empty, but beyond in the first coach he came to, were the sounds of restless life. Toward the front, a baby cried. There were protests from those trying to sleep nearby: "Calm that baby down." "Rock it — rock it!" And a mumbled response from the mother, frustrated, doing her best.

Lucky me — back in my room where the only sound is the train rumbling along and sleep is easy.

Here this young mom could probably have slept a week, but between her baby and coach seat neighbors, she had nothing but noise and complaints. Couldn't blame the neighbors either – we all tend to get a bit grumpy when kept up.

He didn't feel like going any further forward but turned and headed back toward the sleeping cars. Passing through the diner, sadness struck him. All these empty tables and dim light, when only a few hours before it had been animated by travelers eating together and sharing talk — almost like religious pilgrims on the way to a common destination.

When he reached the door at the end of the corridor, he paused. He did not enter the lounge car, but slowly turned, stood for a moment and then headed back toward the front.

What surprised him was how easily she came. Maybe it was just being so uncomfortable with the complaining neighbors that anything seemed better. She was a young Black woman, with that ropey hairstyle he'd seen in the Caribbean.

When they got to the door of his bedroom, she looked him over — assessing how old and harmless he might be. "I have been described as 'a boy you can trust'," he told her.

"I believe it," she said. "'Cepting the boy part."

"Fair enough. You go in first, and I'll help you get settled."

At his direction she crawled into the bed with the baby and took the extra blanket he handed her from the closet. "Thank you, sir." She looked so cozy and settled in, almost asleep already.

"I'm going to sit here on this little seat — in case the porter comes or anything should happen."

"All right," she murmured. "Good night."

He sat and watched, and very soon her breathing was heavy. The baby had not uttered a sound since entering the bedroom, as though he knew that this now was a legitimate sleeping room, no more protest needed.

Good that they had eased into the sleep we all need if we're ever to rise again. Fleeing by the window, the dark trees seemed to gesture with their limbs like vanishing ghosts, until he shut his eyes.

Suddenly awake – with a terrible thought. Actually two. What if, in her tiredness, this young mother had overslept her station? He was sure the train had stopped at least once. Number two: the police might be waiting for him at *his* station. If they had traced him through the credit card, they might have decided not to special-stop the train, with all that delay and bother, but simply post a couple of plainclothesmen at the Fort Lauderdale station gate.

But had she over-slept her station?

"It's morning. Morning time," he murmured, touching her shoulder.

She started and sat up suddenly. "Where are we?"

"I think we might have passed Orlando — is that all right?"

"Oh, sure. We don't get down till Fort Lauderdale."

"Well, that's just fine. We're headed to the same place. Let's go to breakfast in the diner."

He left the room so she could get herself and the baby ready.

They were in the dining car ahead of the rush, just the two of them seated across from each other with the baby in a special little seat the steward had kindly provided. "Sir, really appreciate last night. This little guy and I — we needed that sleep."

The little guy was sucking his thumb and watching Ted carefully with his big dark eyes, like he expected him to do something else surprising at any moment.

"Certainly welcome, but you can drop the 'sir.' I'm just ninety."

She laughed out loud. "How old you have to get before you want the 'sir'?"

He almost blushed. "Don't know. Maybe I'll recognize it when that day comes."

"Last night, problem was this baby boy won't sleep anyways but flat. You saw soon as I put him level on your bed back there, he was happy."

"Yes, that was good to see."

It turned out she lived in North Carolina and was headed to Florida to interview for a college scholarship. Good – he told her the same story he'd used on the college couple last night, as a cover to pay for her breakfast.

"I'm breaking *all kinds of rules* on this train," she told him with mischievous zest. "Last night, sleeping in a first class room on a coach ticket. And you know Amtrak doesn't allow pets in the baggage car anymore, but I've got a dog in the baggage car."

"Oh? Wonder why they changed—"

She shushed him, because the waiter was coming up to take the order.

When that was done, she resumed in the low voice of conspiracy. "I actually broke two rules there. One is what I told you – only guide dogs are allowed and only right next to their blind owners."

"So how did you get him in the baggage car?"

"I said he was the guide dog of my grandma down in Florida, and she needed him. They saw I couldn't manage him and the baby both in the coach, so they found a big crate and put him up front with the trunks."

"So you got him in the baggage car. What other rules did you break?"

"He's no guide dog. Fact is, he's so old and blind, he could use a guide dog his own self."

Before the breakfast came, he began his interview. A private university was considering this girl, Lawanda Tuffet, for a full scholarship, so it was well worth her effort to come down and talk to them. Also, her grandmother lived in the area and could help her take care of the baby if she did win the grant.

"About Beauregard — he's the dog — I don't want you to think I'm a lying, law-breaking type of person," she suddenly interrupted. "It's just I had to get him back to my grandma some way. After getting a ride up, she flew back to Florida, and they wouldn't let her take him on the plane. She's not blind, but she does *need him* — to love. I wasn't lying about that."

He finished the interview, but there was something about that dog he couldn't get out of his mind. "What breed is Beauregard?"

"German Shepherd. He's fat and old and about blind, but you can still tell that."

"Oh, that's interesting. That is very interesting indeed."

So interesting in fact that it led to an improvised wardrobe session in bedroom C, Car 235 before the train arrived in Fort Lauderdale.

So interesting that it resulted in the four of them leaving from the baggage car and starting down the platform together like a family, since an old white-haired white man by himself was what the police would be looking for. They would not be looking for an old white man without obvious hair but a full head of mangoes (the bandana which Lawanda's brother had brought her from a Jamaican holiday), wearing a home-made "Blind" sign and in company with a young mother, her baby and his own seeing-eye dog. He was wearing his very dark sunglasses, to make him look blind, and being led by the leashed Beauregard, who really was blind — the old dog himself being led mainly by the scent of Lawanda in front carrying her baby boy, looking back big-eyed over her shoulder because again something new and surprising was happening.

As a seeing-eye dog Beauregard appeared questionable — wobbling right and left as he lost and regained his mistress's scent. This made it hard for Ted, holding tight to his leash, to keep his balance, being constantly jerked about. "Slow down, sir," he commanded the dog. "Remember yourself, sir!" But the elderly Beauregard, in apparent fear of losing his mistress, kept careening this way and that. Ted dearly hoped that any watchful police weren't experts on canine leaders of the blind.

"Aaaugh!" he cried out.

Beauregard had crashed into a small cardboard trash container, knocking it directly in front of Ted — who had tripped and gone sprawling onto the platform.

"Oh, grandfather — you all right?" Lawanda, come to help. He took a moment to breathe, then took her arm to rise — shoving his dark glasses back on, while Beauregard was barking furiously at this affront, challenging all comers.

"M'am, please to restrain that dog."

A big policeman had put a hand on Ted's shoulder. So it hadn't worked, the disguise. They had him, he thought with despair.

"Sorry, he's just old and jittery."

The big policeman stared hard at Ted. "*This dog* going to guide you? He looks most blind himself."

Ted nodded sadly, making a conscious effort to gaze off like a blind man. "Yes, he's old, like me. But you get attached. Don't want to put him out of work for some new hotshot dog fresh out of training school."

"Sir, I understand how that is. I'm local police, and I just wanted to issue a warning. We've had a gang of bad kids around here beating up on the handicapped and old. So don't be out on the street where there's no one else around."

"Oh, that's all? Well, thank you officer."

"You sure you all right after that fall?"

"At the moment I'm feeling fine!"

So their little family procession continued unmolested down the platform and into the station, though Beauregard crashed two more times, and they had to drag him away from where he was furiously challenging a mop and pail, and later a waiting room vending machine.

Then Ted stepped out onto the sidewalk and felt the sun. *The old person's dream, to be enfolded in the warmth of youth.*

He shared a cab with Lawanda, little Shawn and Beauregard. She gave the driver her grandmother's address, and he asked to be dropped first at the main downtown office of his bank, so to make the game as soon as possible.

As they drove, he asked what she most wanted out of the university, if she did win the scholarship. To study city planning and design housing for the working poor, she told him with enthusiasm – not just attractive buildings but true communities that fostered belonging and neighborliness.

"How did you discover this?" he asked her. "Summers I volunteered at social work non-profits or interned with city planning departments. That was part of it." She hesitated. "But I think actually it was more from reading my favorite author, Charles Dickens."

"Really!"

"Oh, yeah. He shows so clear the cruelty and corruption of London, but also the hope in those quirky, interesting people — the city waiting to be born for them, gleaming on a hill!"

"Very glad for you. To have vision like that … a lot of folks would die for."

The cab had stopped. This must be the bank.

"It's been good to know you in this world, Mr. Ted Not-Old-Enough-To-be-A-Sir-Yet. I always will remember you."

"And be sure you will not be forgotten by Theodore Costas," he told her, as he handed the cabbie enough dollars to cover the fare to her grandmother's house, with tip. "You're a spunky young woman, with a hopeful vision that's so good to see."

This ought to work, he thought as he reached the grand front entrance, because it was the same bank he used back home. It had better – the whole plan depended on it.

"I don't have my check book," he told the teller, "but I want to do a withdrawal. Here's my account number, and here's my driver's license."

He looked them over. "So you're from Maryland." That seemed somewhat to displease him. He squinted at the license photo, then at him.

"The dark sunglasses — I can't see your eyes."

"Oh, I'm sorry. And I should have taken off this bandana too. A mango-head is not my natural cranium."

Once he had slid it off his scalp, letting his hair pop up, and removed the glasses, the man seemed to better like his looks. "All right, sir. I'm going to write down the license number. Here's a withdrawal slip for you to complete."

When Ted passed it back to him, he scowled again. "That's a lot of money to withdraw."

"Yep, but you check it, and you'll see it's all sitting in that account right this minute, not doing a thing in this world."

The teller did that, pecking away at his computer, and then he went and had a whispered conference with another man. Ted tried to stop fidgeting — he didn't want to make them more suspicious, and the whole thing depended on getting his money.

At last the man came back and said he needed to ask him a couple of security questions that were attached to the account. For a scary few seconds, Ted couldn't recall the name of his first pet, but then it came to him and he was all right. The teller relaxed and counted out the bills before him and put them in an envelope.

Outside he found a cab, and twenty-five minutes later he was at the stadium.

He had read the place was old and creaky, but it was a case of love at first sight. He walked up a ramp under hanging palm fronds and found his seat in one of the upper grandstand rows, under a roof in the reduced rate section for Seniors.

Already the second inning, but no matter. It was just being there — like that boy in the hospital had said. He gazed onto the sun-resplendent infield green, wrapped in the golden diamond of the base path. Around that jewel this pristine white baseball was tossed with graceful nonchalance by young men of talent.

And here he was, wrapped in a late happiness.

Beyond worrying about discovery now —this was too good. So he introduced himself to his neighbors:

a sixtyish couple, Manny and Sharon from Pikesville, and a grandfather and grandson, Bill and Kevin from Cockeysville. And two eighty-something ladies, Liz and Bess, who lived in Baltimore City proper, as he did.

As they watched, a promising rookie, whom Manny described as "the phenom of training camp" ingloriously stuck out, and the crowd groaned.

"The life of a phenom is not a happy one," Grandfather Bill said.

That led to an animated discussion of early promise in baseball, and caused Ted to turn away from the action on the field to listen, which is what left him vulnerable. He saw it coming at the last second, sensed the people ducking, felt his neighbor's hand pushing him toward safety.

The ball missed him by a foot, crashing into the seat behind.

He was gratefully thanking Manny for pushing his head safely away, but now that head was swimming. He'd had a scare – heart beating fast, and all these kindly seated neighbors had gone fuzzy, vision blurred.

The Way ahead you cannot see.
Driving blind, you'll pay the piper.
To clear the way for you and me,
Install a Dunst windshield wiper!

"Usually the screen protects these seats" – Liz, in a raspy voice. "But once in a while the ball just curves real sharp and comes in here at us."

Her friend Bess patted him. "That must have been scary for you."

"I am a little dizzy, thank you. Think I'll be all right."

They were watching him, and Manny offered to go get him a coke as a pickup. "Thanks, but I'm better. Guess I dodged a bullet."

Abruptly, a gentleman with a head shaved perfectly bald two rows down turned around and told how a batted ball had hit him in the head when he was a ten-year-old pitcher. "Cut my scalp. They had to take me to the hospital for stitches. Insisted on shaving my whole head first."

A thoughtful silence followed, in which you could sense the unasked question: Was that why he kept his head completely shaved now, out of some perverse revenge at that hospital of maybe fifty years ago?

Gradually, the game became uninteresting as to result — the poor old Orioles had lost all chance of winning — but within it there were moments of baseball beauty. The players seemed to cavort with touching intensity, and often with grace. *Maybe the best we can do*, Ted thought, *cavort with grace in a game we know is lost?*

Now, nearing the end of the game, he had an idea to draw everyone in. "Here's one for us all," he announced: "Think of the first strong memory you have of a game — baseball or softball, playing it or watching it, any level."

Right away he could sense that folks were going to run with this. Manny's wife Sharon was the first one in, amusing everyone with the story of how she was so unconfident as a hitter on her first softball team that she would be up a tree whenever her turn in the batting order came: "When I saw the girl ahead of me go up to the on-deck circle, I would start climbing."

A man seated near the end of the row leaned forward and told them how as a teenager he'd seen Babe Ruth hit a home run. "He was fat and over the hill, playing in his last year, but he was Babe Ruth, and I knew I'd never forget seeing that as long as I lived. I can see it now."

Others recounted memories they seemed to savor, lighting up the eyes of the tellers and maybe explaining why they were here so many decades later, seeking to connect this present to the world of that time.

A man from the row behind told the story that finished it. In high school he had been playing in a postseason tournament, in a game that had turned ugly — players and coaches baiting each other and going after the umpires on every close call. But in the next to last inning something very different occurred. The seventeen-year-old version of himself was playing left field, the score was tied and the other team had the bases loaded. One of their guys hit a screaming line drive to his right, and it skipped past him just fair. It was obvious all three runners were going to score, but suddenly he heard the umpire yell "Foul ball!"

The opposition coaches went rabid, rushing out to protest. They asked the other umpire to consult, but to no avail — he hadn't been in position to see it.

"Our main coach," the man went on, "was a quiet fellow and hadn't been a part of all the baiting and getting on the umps. Suddenly I saw him stand up in the dugout and start walking down the left field line toward me. To this day I can picture him coming, unhurried and sure in what he was doing. And I can hear his voice asking me, 'Sammy, you were the closest — did you get a good look at that ball?' 'Yes, sir,' I said. I mean this was a man you always told the truth to. 'It was a fair ball.' 'That's what I thought,' he said, turned and walked back in that same deliberate way.

"He called over the head umpire, and the opposition coach who was going after him — all red-faced and furious, cussing and kicking dirt — and he spoke very calmly to them. I can remember this exact, because I had followed along behind him, knowing this was something I should hear. He said, 'Gentleman, my left fielder was within twenty feet of where that ball hit, and he told me it was fair. Our team accepts those three runs as legitimate.' That little red dog coach's jaw dropped open, the umpire waved the runs in, and we ended up losing. But I'm here to tell you the one remaining inning of that game was played in a different world. By what he had done, that man had changed the world it was played in.'"

Ted knew that would be the last story, because it was *the* story. It told of what people wanted to do for this bloody world from the truth in their hearts, but hardly ever did.

What they did instead was make up jingles. They didn't have to be in advertising, like he had been. Everyone recited everyday jingles, even if they rarely rhymed, to sell and defend the self-product, and to anyone who would listen — how our foul balls were really fair. We made of life one long ad campaign of song and dance, gossip and slogan, all aimed at finding customers who would buy us.

Lying in that hospital bed, before he'd thought of this escape, he had written in his head one last jingle — the song he had sung all his life to sell the most personal product of all.

It's me again for your approval.
I'm the one you've got to see.
Deny me and risk your own removal
So sign off on me, sign off on me.

The game was ending, and his fellow seniors were teasing about who was "going down to run." Seemed to be a tradition here – to end the spring season with a 'Seniors Run the Bases Day,'"

Perfect, Ted thought. *This way I can manage it better for everyone.* "We've got to do this!" he cried. "Please, everyone come down with me."

"The only way I'm going is if they have ambulances and emergency meds stationed everywhere," Manny said.

"You don't really have to run," Liz reminded him. "Just keep moving."

"This will likely be my last game," Ted told them. "I'd take it as a personal kindness if you all would join me on the field of play."

He went first, others promising to follow. Turned out there were no ambulances, as Manny had joked, but an official was passing out warning statements.

Ted started down the baseline toward first, the leader of the pack. He tried going beyond a walk into an actual run, or as close as he could still get to one. Turned out to be a sort of hobble step, but he was bouncing a little, so it might qualify as a jog. No denying he was inspired.

Pretty confident rounding first base, but before he reached second he slowed to a brisk walk — more out of breath than he'd realized. Passing second, he flicked sweat from his forehead, felt dizzy. He had the odd sensation of not minding the strains of his body due to the cloud of images rising in his mind.

That girl he'd had slight, unhappy contact with in high school but met on that train platform in Ashland seventy years ago — now she seemed to be waiting for him again with her patient boyfriend near third base, smiling with anticipation for their resuming that college age conversation in which they had forgiven themselves their competitive foolishness of two years before... yet now he saw that the faces were those of that college couple he had treated in the dining car who were headed home to Savannah, and now a policeman came toward him — and was that Robyn behind him, waiting to have him arrested so she could commit him to the Shangri La Senior Spa? But here was Lawanda with her dog, and she would not allow him to be taken: at a signal from her, Beauregard confronted the policeman as fiercely as if he had been a belligerent vending machine or mop in a pail.

"Sir, you might oughta rest a minute — don't overdo it now," the policeman was saying, so there was no Robyn really, and he didn't need rescuing by Lawanda and dog. No, he saw that the man was no policeman but only a stadium usher. And he did slow down — had to now because of the dizziness, although through it he saw a scared Babe Ruth starting to climb a tree because it would soon be his turn at bat. No, that couldn't be Ruth — now he was really mixing up. *Doesn't matter, all our same stories.*

And there ahead of him at home plate stood Estelle! Oh, that wifely smile after these years apart, welcoming him home. He did succeed in stepping on the plate before he went down before her. Breathing hard, but on his knees now it was better, and he began to reach into his pocket, pulling out the bills and handing one to each person coming toward him. Each took it with surprise, even awe. He had intended to say something of reassurance to each at the time of giving, but he could no longer remember what, and he had no breath for speaking. But Estelle understood just what he was doing, better than she ever had.

And here was that hospital boy, and he would give enough that this twelve-year-old could stay all week watching the games in that special world a boy could make in his mind.

So good now that he could keep peeling one hundred dollar bills from his right thigh to bless all comers. Perfect, like … the joy of man's desiring.

Out near the pitcher's mound a gray shape was looming above all the ordinary human ones. He was twelve feet tall, everyone gazing up at him. It was the coach who had asked his left fielder whether the ball was fair, and then gone and told the umpire the truth — against his own ambition — and thus changed the game forever. Estelle saw it too, realizing everything.

For him it was too late for saintly actions to change the game like that, but at least he could keep peeling this skin off his right thigh, layer by layer for all these others reaching home ... until there would be nothing left of him to give away.

4

"Mystery solved," Robyn told her apartment mate, Mildred. "It came to me last night. Until then, it was like nothing he did in those thirty-four hours after he escaped from the hospital made any sense at all."

"I think it's very sad," the mousy one said. "Is there going to be a funeral? I know with very old people like that often there are so few surviving friends and relatives that —"

"Right, we could have skipped that because he had no family left except us. But his church is insisting on having a service. Otherwise, I could have just let the crematorium finish things up."

The phone rang and Robyn went to answer. It was her lawyer getting back to her. He told her that in his opinion she would have a good case for damages against the Orioles as well as the hospital. He estimated that a quite good settlement could be reached with both.

She put down the phone in an improved mood, and smiled grimly at Mildred. "So all that trouble he went to — escaping the hospital, walking through the cold, taking a long train ride and going out there on the field after the game like a fool with other old folks to run around the bases like he was twelve again — him with a known cardiovascular condition. I kept asking myself why."

"But, from what you told me, the most peculiar thing was him giving away all that money to perfect strangers. That's what—"

"At a bank down there he withdrew ten thousand dollars from his account. In one hundred dollar bills. It seems that down on that field he was giving away one to every person he could get to."

"So that would be for … a hundred people?"

"That must have been his *plan*. Luckily he passed out before he could do that. Gave away about thirty, because the police found nearly seven thousand dollars still in his pocket."

Mildred was shaking her head in wonder.

"Completely crazy — right? But last night it came to me in bed : *It's simple — he did that for the same reason he took an expensive sleeper down there and gave to strangers on the train. It was to spend as much as possible before he died — to keep it away from me!*"

"Well," Mildred said. "But at least you will inherit some—"

"Oh don't worry about Robyn. There will be a whole lot more coming to me now than just what he left."

She began tenderly stroking the old cat beside her on the sofa. "It's just that I'm a person who is curious about life. When I don't understand something, it bothers me. But now the mystery of that old man's crazy behavior is cleared up, and I can get on with the important things."

Chapter Two:
Further Adventures of
Lawanda Tuffet

The old man who had taken care of her and little Shawn on the train had also paid the driver before he left the taxi at his downtown Fort Lauderdale bank, so all Lawanda had to do now that the cab had stopped in front of her grandmother's little stucco bungalow was to get out. That was all, she told herself — just get out. And with her ten month old in one arm, and her blind old German shepherd straining at his leash now — having decided to bark fiercely at the cab driver the moment he opened the back door, though he'd been perfectly fine with him as the driver in front. And then there was the suitcase and diaper bag. Just get out — that was all.

"Here — I'll take the two bags," the cabbie said. "You want them on that front porch?"

"That will do fine, I thank you." Stepping into the heat with Shawn and Beauregard, she wondered vaguely whether the man was treating her better for the fact that it had been another white man who had paid the fare and his tip. The thought made her tired, made her realize she was over-all tired and deserved to be, having slept maybe three hours all last night — after that old man had rescued her and little Shawn from the coach where the baby wouldn't settle down and put them in the real horizontal bed in his own sleeper room.

But she was looking forward to seeing Granny Tuffet. She rang the bell, glad for the cover of the porch roof from the hot and humid midday sun, glad for the smell of the flowers Granny had growing on the porch trellis and really glad for the dim back bedroom where she would soon be napping with the baby. Meantime Beauregard would be sleeping at the feet of Granny T, reunited with his mistress, on the braided rug in the front room.

She rang the bell again. The small window beside the door showed little of the dark room beyond, making instead a mirror in which Lawanda studied herself. Granny didn't approve of her dreadlocks, but otherwise she looked okay, and she had dressed conservative for her and the train.

The bell was working, as she had heard it ring, but maybe not loud enough for a deep-in-sleep grandma. Lawanda went to pounding the door.

Long seconds passed and no sound from inside. Now she had a sudden mind-picture of Granny T, lying diagonal across her bed as she had fallen at the moment of the stroke, her mouth open below the bunned-up hair as though astonished that she — energetic at seventy-two — could so succumb in a moment. How long would she have been lying there but not there?

"Quiet, baby boy — I got to think!"

What to do next?

She was just scaring herself with that picture: Granny T was likely not lying dead inside her house. So the question was had she just got a little mixed up on the arrival time from the train, or had she got very mixed up and gone off to stay over at the house of some friend or family, like she was always doing? If the first was true, she might show up here any minute, but if it was the second she could be gone for days. And she was capable of the second — Lawanda knew her memory wasn't what it used to be. And if her grandma had gone away, what would *she do* with the little money she had — to pay for a motel, feed herself and the baby, get to her interview in the morning, back to the train and anything else?

Now she was watching a mail truck come down the block, knowing that mattered before she could think why.

It was stopping before every mailbox on the street, but would it stop for this one? If it didn't — with all the junk mail that usually came — that could be a big hint.

As it approached, she tied Beauregard's leash around a porch railing and headed toward the street with Shawn.

The truck rolled right by the mailbox, and now she was jogging after it. "Hold it, Sir — just a minute please!"

The driver was a chubby, middle-aged Black man, and he stopped to let her come up. "Excuse me, but I just arrived here, and I'm afraid my grandma got mixed up and left town on me."

He was watching her carefully. This one was into protecting himself, she thought.

"I noticed she didn't get mail today, and I'm wondering if that's because she put a stop delivery at the post office until she gets home."

He was shaking his head definitively. "They don't tell the carriers that. And if knew there was a stop on it, I couldn't tell *you*."

"Oh, why...?"

"You don't look like a house-breaker, but if you was ... That'd be the perfect inside information you'd want to have, now wouldn't it?"

"I see."

The driver started to pull away, but she shouted, "Where is the closest post office?"

"Up to Everglades." He pointed in the direction he had come from. "Then left. But they won't answer that question for you either."

Lawanda sighed, starting to perspire in the sun. She went back to the porch and sat in the shade to cool down and think. "Hush up, Beau — he's gone now!"

Chances are it was not any coincidence that no mail had been delivered. Chances are Granny T. did put in a stop at the P.O. because she was known to have done that before. If so, she was going to be out of town for a while, having completely forgot about her granddaughter coming to stay while she interviewed at the university for the scholarship she would need to go there.

But to be sure of that she ought to walk through this heat to the post office and ask. Might be against regulations, but she would explain why she needed to know. Most likely they would be sympathetic since she had a baby and needed help. Maybe she could even get a tip there on finding a cheap place to sleep tonight with her baby and her blind old dog. If not, she had maybe forty dollars — what was she going to do!

If she could phone any of Granny T's friends or her church, she could likely find out if she'd gone away, but she didn't know any of the friends' last names, and the church was just a storefront rented out on Sundays — no church office with a secretary to call.

Before leaving the house, she wrote a note saying that she was here and had planned to stay with her, and leaving her cell phone number to call. She stuck the note in the front door.

At least Beauregard settled into an easy walk as they started off. Probably he was glad to be moving again after the train and the cab. It was good to have energy even when you got old — and good to be up for adventure, like that old Mr. Ted from the train. Too bad Mr. Beauregard Tuffet couldn't carry something, as this was hard walking for her with baby, leashed dog, small suitcase and diaper bag, and it was getting hot. Good she'd had enough sense to bring her straw hat against this Florida sun.

Turned out Everglades was some long blocks up, and when she turned into it, there was still no post office in sight. Hot work now. At least she had clean clothes with her to change into for tomorrow's interview. But how would she take care of herself and Shawn and Beauregard until then on the money she had?

It seemed there was no resisting it — she felt herself descending into Sagamore Valley. A place she knew too well and would prefer to spend minimum time in. The name she thought to have heard from some high class resort somewhere, but it described the mood — the more you walked downhill into that valley, the more you sagged.

"You're tired, and this is hard walking in the sun and you have no idea where you or the baby are going to sleep tonight," she told herself, but she knew it was more. In spite of herself, she was thinking again about that Devon. Her own fault to trust him because she had known he was far from grown up, but he was fun and cute and a well- meaning person. Not a reader like her, but she had told herself that would be all right, because he had a gift for making little, tiresome things entertaining, and that was what he would bring to the marriage. And he was going to community college to learn a career for himself, in medical tech. And he did seem all looking forward to getting married when she told him the big news, months before he could see for himself the bigness in the news.

But that was before he got the invitation from his like third cousin to go work for his used car business in Kentucky. Nothing could compete with that. Nothing merely human and ordinary, no matter how big — even six months along.

Lawanda stared ahead through the heat shimmering off white sidewalk — no post office. You could usually spot them by the flag.

The Valley of the Sagamore — she would just have to keep plodding on through it until something came to deliver her. Sometimes it could be a thing as small as a memory that would lift her out of it. But Shawn on her left shoulder, diaper bag clutched in the left hand, suitcase in her right hand along with Beauregard's leash. All that made her arms hurt.

Somehow Devon had come to the decision that a wife was not the thing for a wheeling and dealing "Pre-owned Vehicle Representative". Not for a "PVR" who had been promised that once he got to Kentucky he would be furnished a late model pre-owned himself to sport around in — of course, he couldn't take along any old acquaintances who might distract from the style of that. As best she could read him, this seemed to be it. What it came down to — in his mind that late model pre-owned he'd been promised was just a deal shinier than she was.

At last, here was the post office. But the first look she had of the one clerk was not a promising one: here was one into suspicion of everything, which meant he would follow the rules to protect his butt no matter what.

While she was explaining how it came about that she was stuck here with a baby boy, old blind dog, not much money and no place to sleep before her interview at the University tomorrow and that was why she needed info on whether her granny might be out of town, his expression did not change. He was almost a look-alike to the postal truck driver back there, could've been his brother.

"Sorry, but we don't reveal who has put in Stop Delivery Cards. That's a solid gold rule to protect our customers."

"I understand why that makes sense in general. But she's my grandma — I'm not going to rob her house."

"How do I know that?"

"I got ID, and luck is that she's my *daddy's* mom, so her last name is the same as mine. Here — look at this!"

But the man was shaking his head, refusing even to glance at it. "Family members steal from each other all the time. Don't prove nothing."

This was getting her nowhere. Might as well assume that Granny T was not going to be home and she was not going to be able to stay there.

"That dog is not supposed to be in here either," the man said. "'Less he is seeing-eye, and your eyesight seems plenty good to me."

"What if *he's* blind enough that he could use his own seeing-eye dog? What if, left outside, he would be fierce enough to scare away your customers, having taken them for space invaders? What do the solid gold rules have to say about that?"

He gave her a deadeye stare.

"But you're right — I better get him out. He eats postmen for lunch!"

Looked like a MacDonald's a couple of blocks further on, and she could use a bathroom and to change Shawn's diaper. She plodded on through the Valley of the Sagamore, looking forward to a few minutes of air conditioning in there, trying not to think too much about anything else.

She tied Beauregard to a small tree that had been planted at the edge of the parking lot and took the baby inside. There was a line for the ladies room — teenage girls loud and annoying to wait with. In fact, the whole place was overrun with teenagers, so that she wouldn't want to sit there and eat something and cool off. Save the money — not that much of it anyway.

When she came out again into the heat, some boys were pegging stuff from the garbage container at poor Beauregard, who was rewarding their efforts with ever fiercer barking. "That's enough, Beau!" She got him to stop, and out of the corner of her eye saw the boys go slack-armed and slouch off to some other entertainment.

In the restroom, the idea had come to her to go to the University. After all, she had some credential there — the Dean's letter confirming her interview date tomorrow. From her times of visiting Granny T, she seemed to remember a bus that ran along

Everglades here to downtown, and from there she could probably transfer to another one that would take her out to the University, on the far other side of town. It would take a long time, but she would likely get there. If she paid for a cab, that would leave her too little for motel, buying food or getting back to the train the next day. And if she made it that far, one chance in a million she'd meet someone the quality of that Mr. Ted to help her out, not to mention listen to her soul.

Which reminded her of the strobe she had seen this morning in the dining car. That sudden flash of light showing the bigger picture — whenever she had that, it was salvation for the moment. This particular morning the strobe had shown her that the questions this old man was asking could not be from some standard survey like he told her he was doing. They were too personal, too truly interested not in how she fit into a general pattern but what she was in herself. He must've made up that about a survey as the excuse to pay for her breakfast. For just a minute that strobe had allowed her to see Lawanda Tuffet and the ninety year old white man, Mr. Ted, and the other folks straggling sleepy eyed into the diner in a gracious new light.

There was no bench at the bus stop, so she sat down on a tree stump. Beauregard she got to settle on the grass, slipping her foot through the loop at the end of his leash, to hold him if he suddenly jumped up and began a charge at what he took to be space invaders, like she'd told that post office clerk. Little Shawn turned on her shoulder, and looked up at her, watchful but content. He wasn't worried about when he would eat or where he would sleep but trusted her to take care of him — she always had.

And now she felt herself rising out of the Valley of the Sagamore. It came from remembering that strobe light effect this morning while breakfasting with the old man in the dining car, and now seeing Shawn looking at her this way.

She had named it that to herself this year, because when it came it was like a strobe in turning the surrounding dark of a dance hall suddenly bright, revealing not just yourself going through your little motions but now all the people around in their own dances, each different but connected to yours through the bass rhythm. For that instant you were not only this little dancer in the dark called yourself.

Of course, it was also *not* like a dance hall strobe, because it didn't pulse on and off to any regular beat, but would come upon you unawares, providing only an instant light before it was taken away, leaving you back in darkness. But not quite so blind to what might be hidden as before.

"M'am, we'd like you to come down to the precinct with us."

Lawanda jumped. She had been looking off, watching for the bus, and here this big police cruiser had crept up on her from the opposite direction.

"What about?"

"That old man I saw with you at the Amtrak this morning. Mr. Theodore Costas of Baltimore, Maryland."

"Yes, I do recognize you now," she told him.

"That dog was with *him* then. Supposed to be his seeing-eye dog. Turns out that old man's not blind at all."

She swallowed. They maybe had something on her there. "Of course, I never said he was."

"But you conspired with him to mislead us."

"Well look. Nobody's charged with any crime here — right?"

This big policeman, who had seemed kindly toward Mr. Ted this morning, was squinting tough at her, sitting in the driver's seat. Beside him was a Black man, watching but not talking. "You were involved in a misrepresentation to police. That's an infraction. But we'll overlook that if you cooperate and tell us what you know."

"Okay, good. I'll do that now. There's very little I can tell you."

"We need you to come down to the station, answer some questions and make a statement."

"Wherever you were going on that bus, we'll get you dropped off afterwards," the black cop told her.

Taking her out to the University — that would be a help. She got in their backseat with Shawn, Beauregard, suitcase and diaper bag.

On the way to the station, she asked if Mr. Ted was all right, but they put her off. All the discussion was to be held there, they said. Maybe with recording devices and bright lights in her face — or was she being too dramatic from TV shows?

At the precinct station they left her in a waiting room, and she listened to poor folks seated across from her talking about some lawyer who might be able to "get him off." Their voices had a certain awe whenever they used that lawyer's name: "We get *Harley* for that, it's a done deal. He don't take nothing from no judge, *Harley* don't."

Lawanda smiled to herself: like *Jaggers* in Dickens a hundred and fifty years ago. If Jaggers was for you, what could be against you?

The big policeman — Sergeant Wallis according to his badge — who had talked to them that morning as they got off the train, led her back into a little room and closed the door. There a younger man immediately started reading her about the possible consequences of making false statements to police, even when you weren't charged with a crime. "So the dining car waiter said you and Theodore Costas of Baltimore, Maryland had a long talk, just the two of you over breakfast."

"That's right. He told me he was doing a survey of college student attitudes and had questions from that to ask me."

"Waiter said the two of you were deep in conversation."

Lawanda attempted a non-committal "yes and no" look. "You mind if I feed this boy his lunch? I think that's why he's starting to fuss."

"Let's put that off till later," the other policeman said.

"Suppose we cut to it" – Wallis, abrupt now. "Costas is a missing person. Wanted in Maryland. We want you to tell us everything you know about where he might have gone after you left him this morning."

Lawanda shook her head. "We didn't talk about that. He told me he had come down here on an impulse like. That he'd always wanted to go to Florida when it was still cold up north. Thought this might be his last chance."

"Look, we know you two left the station in the same cab. You better not be holding out on us now!"

"Not me. The one thing else I know is he had the cab driver drop him at a bank downtown."

"Which bank?"

Lawanda shook her head. "Don't know — I'm not from here. Visited my Granma a few times is all. I can show you the building — near where U.S. One turns downtown."

"That's a start. But we know you were in deep talk with him for at least a half hour at breakfast, so it's hard to believe that you have no more idea of what he was planning to do here."

"Okay — you want to know what he told me? Didn't think you'd care about this, but here it is. That he knew he was going to die soon from one of his fainting spells. Didn't matter — he didn't want to spend his last days sitting like a piece of semi-dead meat under supervision in the crummy nursing home where his relative was going to stick him. Said he was going to make up for his life as an advertising jingle man and speak only the truth and give away every part of him that was any good to anybody who would have it. His words exact – which I will not forget – 'who would have it.'"

Sgt. Wallis pursed his lips. "Nothing about where he was headed?"

"Not a thing."

"Okay. Come show us the bank building, and then we'll drop you off."

On the drive there, they did not object to her feeding Shawn in the back seat. Beauregard would be hungry too, she knew — most of the food she'd left in the little plastic dish in his crate had been uneaten when she and Mr. Ted had got him out of the baggage car this morning. But now, as usual, he just sniffed and moved away with disdain from Shawn's bottles of peas and carrots, corn and tomatoes — way below his gourmet standards.

When she pointed out the bank building which the old man had walked toward, Sgt. Wallis got out to begin his sleuthing right then and there, and the other one drove her on to the University.

"I'm looking for the Dean of Admissions office, Crowder Hall," she told him.

"No idea where that is."

"Wait — she sent me a little campus map." She dug it out and passed it over the seat to him.

When he let her out in front, it was nearly five o'clock and the campus looked deserted – what if it had closed down for the weekend!

But the double doors were not locked, and she got the three of them safely through and down the hall to the Dean's office.

"Oh, thank God you're still here," she burst out to the Dean's secretary. A pale, short-haired woman in her fifties, she looked up startled, and Lawanda thought *she's not about to thank God that I'm here with my whole...retinue.* She knew she better pull out the Dean's letter quick before she was hastily dismissed.

The woman read it twice, as though to be sure it was legit.

"I was to stay with my grandma in town, but she's getting old and likely forgot I was coming.

Don't have the money for motel and everything else, so I didn't know what to do but come here and see if the U. could put us up somewhere until my interview tomorrow morning."

The woman was shaking her head. "It's spring vacation week. The students are gone, and the dorms are locked up tight until Sunday. I don't know what to tell you."

Pretty clear that this woman would come up with no creative ideas to help out. "Can you give me the Dean's home number? I'll ask her what to do."

The secretary remained motionless, as though such an out of the ordinary request had frozen her stiff. At last, she said, "Well, I *guess* I can do that. And then it will be up to her."

The phone rang five times and an answering service clicked on: the Dean's voice, much more pleasant than this woman's, inviting her to leave a message. Lawanda briefly explained her dilemma and left her cell phone number for a call back.

The secretary was getting her things together for leaving. Lawanda felt her heart racing, knew she had to figure this out quick. "Are there vending machines here? The day has gone so strange I haven't had a chance to eat since breakfast."

Yes, there were. One level up, the woman said, then to the right.

"But you've got only twenty minutes or so, before security locks the building up tight, so be sure you get out in time. Being the weekend coming up, even the cleaning crew doesn't come through until tomorrow morning."

Now that is very helpful, Lawanda thought. *Lady, you are the most helpful to me when you're not trying to be.*

One floor up, all she did was check that the vending machines were there — with a changer — because the main thing was to find a small storage type room which they wouldn't be checking for people working late.

What she found was a glorified closet that closed off from a secretary's office. It was a sort of junk and paper supply room — large trash bin, broken swivel chair and some computer paper on the shelves. "Boys, this is just for now," she muttered. "We move into the hotel's master suite, more fitting to our high style, a little later."

Shawn was already asleep and would be for a while. As long as Beauregard kept quiet, they should go undetected. And he wouldn't start to bark unless he heard something very close. Lucky that his hearing wasn't that much better than his seeing.

If the Dean got her message and called her cell phone, likely she would come get her and put them all up somewhere, but she couldn't rely on that. You had to make your own plans for protection, and then if someone did come through for you that was a bonus. Like the ninety year old Mr. Ted Costas, but weren't many like him in the world.

She got a little scared when she heard some muffled male voices coming near, but they drifted away. After that, she gave it another half hour by her cell phone before she peeked into the hall.

Nothing but some mechanical building pops and gurgles.

"Boys, I believe we can now move into more fitting quarters."

It was a little after six, but there was still natural light coming into the halls. Later, it would likely be just some real low emergency lighting that would make it harder to see anything.

The three of them, plus suitcase and diaper bag, moved slowly down the halls until she found what she'd hoped for: an inner office with a couch! No windows was crucial, so no light would show to an outside watchman. The room even had a lamp, so they wouldn't only have the choice of bright fluorescent overhead or darkness. Not a big room, but perfect.

She set up Shawn on a chair cushion in a corner, with his blanket tucked in around him and straight chairs laid flat on their sides to keep him in. He had been dragged around all day, missing his usual nap, so he would be good for hours. Beauregard was already settling himself on a scatter rug across the room.

Out in the hall, she found the vending machines stocked with sweets. "Not good for dog or girl," she murmured. The alternatives were "Cheese Puffins", a sort of bird-shaped cheese thing, and "Dr. Pretzelo", a thick pretzel stick with a little bulging head at the top — eyes, nose and mouth outlined by red salt crystals. She loaded up on both.

Back in the office room, she broke open a package of each, and the food smell brought Beauregard to her at his fastest waddle. She held them out to the old dog, who sniffed once and suddenly appeared quite dejected.

"I know it's not your high cuisine, Beau, but don't turn your nose up so. Look — a genuine Cheese Puffin, whatever that is." He lowered his head dolefully.

"All right then. Here boy — the special for tonight: 'Dr. Pretzelo'! See, here's something you can actually bite its head off!"

But he only licked the salt off it, then waddled sadly away. "Beau, you must be big into avoiding preservatives and achieving balanced nutrition. And here I never suspected you had that turn of mind." She put the rejected Dr. Pretzelo in his dish anyway, in case he got hungry enough.

She had fed Shawn considerable in the cop car coming here, and he wouldn't eat anytime soon. Probably wake up hungry in the middle of the night, but nothing she could do about it.

Maybe Beau needed to drink first. She put the vendo food in a corner, half filled his bowl out at the hall water fountain and set it before him. He lapped it up and then did munch two Cheese Puffins and half a Dr. Pretzelo — slowly, without gusto — before curling up for sleep.

She had to agree with him that these vendo treats were significantly lacking in taste, but it felt good to put something in her stomach and wash it down with a non-caffeine soda, so she could sleep herself before long.

Meantime she dug out her project from the suitcase and practiced how she would present it at the interview tomorrow. When it would start to sound flat and unconvincing in her ear, she thought back to the words she had used to Mr. Ted. They had sure perked him up. He wasn't faking it. A reason she had loved being with him — it really seemed he had got too old for faking.

After a while she switched from the project to the book about how to present at an interview. Here she had to force herself to read. Some of the advice was practical, but as Granny T. would say, "I just don't cotton to it." Somehow all those bright-eyed tips, tricks and techniques to sell yourself — somehow she just didn't cotton to it.

But would she be able to sleep through the night and be sharp enough in the morning to convince them? Without the scholarship, she would be back in Beasley, N.C. checking groceries and taking whatever courses she could afford at the community college. With this long night coming on, it would be easy to lose confidence and sink once more into the Valley of the Sagamore.

`What she needed before sleep was inspiration. From under toiletries in the suitcase, she brought out *Little Dorrit, h*er place marked by an unwritten postcard only a few chapters from the end. So quickly they surrounded her: the grotesque and struggling people, doing comic, passionate and amazing things in a long ago world, turned by imagination into one that — at the deep level that mattered — so resembled her own.

She finished the chapter, but then couldn't resist going back to a previous one to re-read a favorite part. It was the moment when Amy Dorrit, just a young woman of about her own age, at last confronts the old guilty invalid, Mrs. Clennam, who uses religion to justify her keeping money from years before that wasn't hers — justifies it on the basis that God wanted his disciples to be the instruments of punishment to the unrighteous. What a perversion of religion! She relished reading again how Amy, in a purely simple and beautiful way, told the strict old woman how that was not what Jesus was about at all.

And now she could fall asleep, wondering whether in the morning she could express to strangers what she was about at all.

It was the mysterious Floo bird of Florida that they were in pursuit of, led by this little red-faced cracker from Tallahassee, but this was all happening in the remote bush, somewhere in Africa. The cracker, name of Floyd Spivey, was in front wearing a shiny pith helmet and driving the jeep. Next to him sat Granny T in a long white summer dress like she might have worn to a dance in her girlhood. She herself was sitting in the back next to Mr. Ted Costas, now known as "the Great White Hunter". Beauregard and little Shawn had been left for safety in the village with caretakers.

It was getting hot, and she wondered whether this Floo bird pursuit would turn out to be worth it.

"You hear that?" Floyd hissed at them. "Listen up!"

There was an echoing bird sound, as from a great distance: "Floo...floooo!"

"That's him!"

"I don't need to go no further to find some big old bird," Granny T. proclaimed. "The further we go, the hotter it's getting."

"What you expect? That bird is located exact on the e-quator," Floyd said.

Lawanda knew that he himself was none too anxious to get there, as he'd kept telling pieces of native legend to scare them off : if the Floo bird sees you, he will begin to weep buckets of tears at the pitiful sight, and unless you can outrun that flood of his tears, they will freeze you in a grief so large you can never escape it.

But despite his fears and Granny's grousing, they were going on this quest because she and Mr. Ted had heard that if you could once get close enough actually to see the Floo bird, just got one halfway good look at it, you would know forever how to do and stop the foolishness of life forever.

But the louder the bird cries got, the hotter the jungle breath that surrounded them. "Flooo … FllOOOOO!"

"I wished I'd a never come," Granny T. was saying. "Wished I'd a stayed home in my air condition."

"We must be prackly at the e-quator now."

"Just as much as you, I want to learn forever how to do and stop the foolishness," Lawanda said, turning to Mr. Ted beside her. "But I'm sweating me a river — I can't stand this much longer."

But the old man said nothing, his face expressionless, and then she saw that he had stopped breathing and that he was lying back against the cracked leather of the seat, passed on forever from this world.

She woke up sweating. Tried to take a deep breath and realized this air was too hot to breathe in. They were practically suffocating in here. Open a window! But there were none in this room — she had to get them all to a window. She grabbed up Shawn from the chair and shouted to Beau.

Staggering out into the hall, she found it only slightly cooler. She had to get them to a room with a window that opened. Once the air conditioning was turned off, the heat must have just kept mounting while they slept.

The baby felt damp against her shoulder like he had sweated too and Beau was sort of staggering behind her, but she pressed ahead in the sweltering air, looking for a room with a window. But what if they wouldn't open because the building depended only on its air conditioning? Horrible thought.

They'd have to go outside even if the door alarm went off, alerting a watchman. But what if the doors were chain-locked — horrible thought number two! They had to have air!

By just these low amber wall lights set above the floor, she was looking for any room with an open door — the two closed doors she'd tried had been locked from the hall.

An intersecting corridor, and she took it to the right because she felt the main entrance would be that way. And now a large office opened out to the left. Across the carpet there were windows, but would they open? Standing for a second before that promise of air, she allowed herself one breath, one quick prayer, before she turned the hand crank and pushed down hard. It gave, and then she was pushing the window out, and the one on each side of it as well. Three open windows, thank God!

She held the baby to the opening. A little breath of air, a little breath of life, thank God.

It was only later after they had all cooled down a little and her panic subsided that she remembered that this second floor was the highest in the building, and therefore would be hottest. The day's sun heat collected in the attic would have been baking down through the ceiling into this level, and hot air couldn't sink into cooler air on lower floors. She should have thought of all that, and settled them — once Security had locked up the building and left — down in the first floor or even the basement if there were finished rooms down there. A big mistake.

"We're going to move again, guys," she told them.

They pressed on down the hall, found a stairs, descended two flights and found it much cooler. Shawn was whiny and Beau was sluggish, but she found a low lit bathroom where she gave the boy a sponge bath to cool him down and poured two paper cups of water on the old dog's back. He gave a short startled bark, but then responded with a wag of the hindquarters. She filled his bowl and Shawn's bottle, changed the boy's diaper and drank three cups herself of the water of life.

Further along the basement corridor, she found a bare room, but it did offer a clean carpet to sleep on. Her cell phone said it was midnight.

She fed Shawn some peas and carrots, Beau chewed up two Dr. Pretzillos, she ate a Cheese Puffin, and then they all lay themselves down to sleep.

Lying there prone on the floor with a fat book for her pillow, Lawanda felt this unknown cellar enfolding them in its cooler, damper breath. *We will go with this, put our trust here*, she thought, *to get us all to morning.*

This time it was no dream — Lawanda was yanked from sleep by a man shouting at her from a fierce face behind blinding flashlight with a pistol pointed at her eyes. He had that savage look of a human roused to violence.

Too asleep to fully feel the fear, she thought almost dreamily, *the attack signal he's wearing on his face— the rage and fear before we do to someone. But please don't do to us!*

"It's just me!" she cried, thinking *that makes no sense but doesn't have to if it reaches him.*

"I'm just a mom who had to sleep here before my interview with the Dean tomorrow because I didn't have any other place I could afford" — beginning to say the words faster now as she felt her own fear coming on. "Would you like to see my letter? It's an invitation from Dean Smithers."

He lowered the gun. It might be all right.

"Hand it over here."

He was a security guard, and Lawanda realized he must have seen the windows she'd left open at that hot room upstairs — or maybe opening them had set off some security warning — and then he had hunted them down.

"Beau, give it a rest! He's just a blind old dog, scared of everyone really," she told the guard. She got the letter out of her bag and handed it to him.

He stepped back to check it out by flashlight.

"You got ID?"

"Coming right up."

It took him just a minute to match the name on the license to the name on the letter, and the photo to her face. "All right, Miss Tuffet. Sorry to come in on you like this. But I didn't know who might have broken in here." He was a nice looking young black man now that his face had relaxed.

"I didn't break in. We just hid and stayed here when the building was locked up. Didn't have the money for a motel, and you can't beat the overnight rate here."

While he went to the far wall and threw on a light switch, she explained about missing connections with Granny T because her memory was going.

"Oh yeah. I got a couple of old ones like that in my family too."

That simple remark turned out to help her after he left, helped her avoid the sense that she would never get back to sleep now and would arrive at the interview too exhausted to give them thoughtful answers, too drained to give them passion. But this man's connection to what she had told him and his bit of a smile — that had given her just a touch of the strobe light, illuminating the big picture where you could see how all the little stories connect. Holding back the darkness of the Valley Sagamore.

It was four-fifteen A.M. How long now would it take her to wind down and sleep again? She had been tired anyway from last night in the day coach before Mr. Ted had rescued them, and now these violent sleep interruptions.

She set her cell phone alarm for 8:30, knowing she might need an hour and a half to get herself alert, washed and dressed in fresh clothes, take Beau out to do his business and diaper and feed Shawn. For now, she would do her very best to make her mind a blank, so that it couldn't race with worries or excitement about this interview at ten, however important to her future.

"Make your mind a blank, girl," she murmured. "Pray for peace."

2

Dean Smithers got to her office early because she was nervous about the phone message left by the scholarship applicant. She and her husband had been out late the night before, and she hadn't bothered to check the answering service until morning. The message went in and out of clarity, but she gathered that this Lawanda Tuffet, who was scheduled for the ten o'clock interview, had somehow missed connections with the relative she was to stay with and was asking for help. The phone number she had left wasn't clear, so she hadn't been able to call even this morning to check on the girl. And now it was 9:55, and she still hadn't arrived, though applicants usually came early for these full scholarship interviews.

Her interoffice rang, and Mrs. Bross told her that Professor Regnand of Planning and Development had just shown up.

"Please tell him to come in."

The door opened and Regnand entered, followed by Professor Spruce of the English Department, who had also been invited.

"Morning, gentlemen. You know each other?"

"Oh yeah, Sprucey and I have been on a couple of committees."

The Dean indicated a couch opposite, and before the men even sat told them, "I'm a little worried about our applicant. I got an unclear phone message that something had gone wrong."

Spruce groaned. "So we might have to sit around. You know I question whether I can add much here for a Planning student. I know you like to have someone from English if the application claims interest in literature, but you know that's generally puffery."

"That's why we include you, Sam. To find out if that's what it is."

"Does that happen a lot?" Regnand asked.

Spruce rolled his eyes. "I think these high school guidance counselors tell half the students to put down something about how much they appreciate 'English literature'. You see all the old standard writers mentioned, but the favorite is Shakespeare."

"And that turns out to be phony?"

"Oh yeah. They've read a few plot summaries, and sometimes memorized a line or two, but they rarely understand what it means. Last year a student applicant comes in here, says he loves Shakespeare and quotes us what he says is a favorite line, 'Romeo, Romeo, wherefore art thou Romeo?'"

"Yeah?"

"It's true that 'wherefore' is obsolete, but if you have actually read the play, you remember from the context that Juliet is not asking anything about *where*. She is asking *why* are you, Romeo, fated to be from a family I can't marry into? With likely some deeper implications about his identity in her question."

"I might not have gotten that."

"Right, but you're not selling yourself as a Shakespeare lover who has recently read the play, and for whom that is a favorite line. So I asked the student the meaning of that 'wherefore art thou Romeo'? and he answers, 'Juliet is asking Romeo where he's at.'"

They all laughed, but then the Dean checked her watch. "It's five minutes after. Applicants are usually on time. This has me worried."

Professor Spruce twisted in his chair: "Has Admissions considered giving these Scholarships for the Disadvantaged simply on the basis of being disadvantaged? Plus school grades and the SAT — to show whether they can do the work? I mean why not just cut out this interview stuff?"

The Dean was shaking her head slowly. "We would lose some human aspect in evaluating. We're trying to find something special in these students. Looking for those who would be especially served by what we offer and would then go on especially to serve the world."

"Serving the world is all very well," said Regnant, looking at this watch. "But I too have a very busy morning."

<u>**3**</u>

When she woke, it felt like she'd been out a long time. Shawn was whining, and he usually slept in pretty good.

She grabbed at her cell phone: God — it was 9:49!

Its alarm had totally failed her, or had she been so tired as to set it wrong, or sleep through it? She had exactly eleven minutes to get upstairs for the interview!

It all rushed at her: *Get yourself dressed in the fresh clothes and halfway decent looking, diaper Shawn — you'll have to feed him during the interview. Tie Beau up on the concrete over there, so if he goes it won't ruin the carpet. Then get upstairs and just tell them what happened.*

The "just tell them what happened" stayed with her, helping her do it. At 10:11 she entered the Dean's outer office, surprising that dead-eye secretary who had been no help yesterday — surprised likely because she had already counted her out as a shiftless no-show. But she would just tell them what happened.

Something she had taken from Mr. Ted Costas, from when he told her that he had gotten too old for anything but the truth. And he had said she had spunk and vision, and on a good day maybe she did.

There were three of them in the inner office — the lady Dean who had invited her and two male professors. The Dean had a plain open face that at least looked glad to see her.

"So sorry to be late," she told them. "But I do have a story to tell, though I'll give you the short form. Excuse me feeding this boy — you'll hear why I have to do it now."

She did give them the short version, beginning with missing sleep on the train and Granny T's absence — but skipping the police pickup — and giving them a picture of the crazy night she had spent in the building. "I had set my cell phone for 8:30, but either it didn't go off or I was too far under to hear it. I woke up eleven minutes to ten, and that's why this boy's not fed and I'm not more together myself. Oh, maybe the janitor should be told that my Granny's old blind German Shepherd is tied up in a little alcove in the basement — outside Room 017. He barks a lot but not much bite left even if he had the inclination, which he doesn't — crazy old sweet pie."

Professor Regnand of the Planning and Development Department — the one she was hoping to major in — started in questioning her while she was spooning the corn and tomatoes into Shawn's little craw. The man had big, bony brows which seemed to focus his dark eyes down on what was directly before him – in this case asking why she had done as many summer internships in social work as in planning departments.

"Honestly, sir, I don't believe in pure design solutions to human problems. That's the truth of it."

"Please say more."

"Well, it's odd and cranky human beings I most want to design communities for. They're single moms like me and drug abusers, teenagers looking out for gangs to connect to, folks that don't have much education but, sometimes, a lot of anger. I just believed that to design communities for them I would need to find out everything I could about their lives — from social services, police, public health, church volunteers, demographers. You name it, and we can use it in design."

"Fair enough." This prof no longer stared straight down at his notes but was now looking up at her, which she took as a good sign. "However, do you have any concepts yourself at this point that you would want to incorporate? I believe you wrote of a plan for a new inner city development in subsidized housing?"

"Right. I think it all should be out in the open — in front of God and everybody. No back alleys, no back ways in. Of course, rear fire doors. But everyone comes through one front plaza to enter a building. The grandmas can watch over the kids playing there and the teenagers, the police can watch over any drug dealers trying to congregate. It's the development's front yard where everyone plays, gets to know each other and brings stuff out in the open. Things don't go down without being known. Not saying I understand all how to do that, or there aren't other design considerations, but I think you've got to inspire people with the chance for a true and responsible community life. Or they won't take care of it, and it will be just more of scared people shrinking."

At least this Planning professor was nodding thoughtfully, like he was giving her idea respect. She had finished feeding Shawn, so she could set him down on the carpet now with his favorite three page plastic picture book and a ball he liked to roll.

"Here, let me show you my perspective drawing for that plan." She took it from the bottom of the suitcase and unfolded it on the Dean's little table. They all three grouped in around her and studied it. This professor Regnand asked her a couple of basic questions, and then suddenly commented: "Your figures are very interesting."

"Oh, which? The floor area ratios?"

"No. I mean the actual people you've drawn there walking the sidewalks and sitting in the plaza. They don't look like planner drawing figures."

She thought he looked quietly pleased, and decided to press ahead. "You're right, sir. I always think when I see those slender, perfectly dressed shapes gliding along with complete cool in planner drawings — I want to say, 'Wait — stop! Are any real people going to live here? The ones I see in life are often fat or shabby, with twisted up bodies sometimes, sad or mad looking a lot of the time. What if we build for real people like them!'"

They all liked that, and Lawanda felt herself getting a second wind. This was going to be fun, trying out on them what she believed. *Thank you, Mr. Ted Costas, for that "no time left for anything but the truth!"*

"That man who did great designs in Chicago and D.C. a hundred years ago, Daniel Burnham, I like what he said: 'Make no little plans. They have no power to stir men's blood.'"

"I've always liked that too," Regnand said. "Now the other prof turned toward her, a narrow chested man with a nervous unsettled style. It seemed he was from a different department, not Planning and Development — why was he here?

"Miss Tuffet, your application claims that you've been inspired in all this by the works of Charles Dickens." He even spoke in a kind of strained, hungry voice.

"Yes, he's my favorite writer."

"Indeed." The man put his lips together in an odd way.

She nodded.

"Well, in this Dickens interest, has it been the TV Christmas Carol presentations, or the BBC adaptations of the longer works, some of the movie versions — what specifically?"

"Oh, no. Some of those are pretty good, but never as good as reading the novels."

"Ummm. Which have you read?"

"Oh, about all of them, except some of the minor things."

"What do you consider 'minor'?"

"Well, I haven't read *Sketches by Boz, Barnaby Rudge* or *The Mystery of Edwin Drood*. I guess the last because it's unfinished, and I was afraid it would leave me... feeling unfinished."

"You're telling me you've read, page by page, even the big novels like *Nicholas Nickleby, Dombey and Son, David Copperfield, Bleak House, Little Dorrit* and *Our Mutual Friend*?"

"Sure. I've read most of those twice."

She had the impression he was astonished, or maybe still not quite believing her.

He cleared his throat. "Well, tell us how they inspire you in your contemplated career ...as an urban planner."

Lawanda gave herself a minute on this, even though she had the impression this prof was looking more suspicious the longer she took. "I think it's how he treats the difficult parts balanced with the possibilities of life," she said and paused. "He knows it's hard, he has great compassion for what people have to struggle with — and not just poor people, though that's more obvious in his books. He understands the struggles of the rich as well – Eugene Wrayburn and Lady Dedlock to name a couple. So he shows the need for compassion, but he doesn't confuse that with 'anything goes', like some modern writers. He knows that evil and sin are real and need to be fought."

The man was watching her now with a narrowed, almost pained look that she didn't understand.

"And he loves the precious peculiarities of people," she went on. "And he relishes their joy when it comes, making it so much fun to enter into.

"More than anything though — to answer your question — I guess what inspires me in my hopes for better urban development is that he shows the hidden goodness in most people. It's just waiting to be brought out somehow! Think about Sidney Carton for instance — a lost, sarcastic drunk until he found a person to sacrifice for. Or Newman Noggs, the bullied servant of Ralph Nickleby — though he is comical! — who conspires to expose his boss and make everything right. Or Panks, the puffing "steam engine" in *Little Dorrit* who seems the harshest bill collector for old Casby, but when he gets the chance, helps those same poor and exposes his boss, and earlier worked his butt off to free the Dorrits from debtor's prison. Or even really minor characters — do you remember in *Hard Times* the unnamed man in a drunken sleep in the country near where poor Stephen is found barely alive at the bottom of the abandoned mine, and who sobers up quick for the emergency and, Dickens tells us, 'becomes the best man of all'? So, more than anything, it's that hidden good he finds in people that inspires me."

This unknown professor started to speak, stammered once, and then her cell phone rang. "Excuse me," she said. "I'm sorry."

But when she heard Granny T's voice, she wasn't sorry at all. She had come home this morning and found the note Lawanda had left stuck in her front door and was apologizing so for having forgotten the day of her arrival. "My friend got a car. We come get you wherever you're at."

"Don't worry yourself with what happened — it's all right. But a pick-up would help. I'm at the U now, doing the interview, and I'll call you back when I'm done. Real glad you're okay and just got mixed up."

She clicked off and looked around at the three of them. "So I guess you figured out that was my granny

I told you about. Like I thought, she just forgot I was coming yesterday."

The questioning professor was giving her an odd look. "Miss Tuffet, I apologize for doubting you. It's just we get a lot of exaggerated claims on these scholarship applications. I'll admit when I read yours I thought someone else might have written it for you, but hearing you talk, now I know better."

She started to tell him it was okay, but he was excited to press on: "Listen, I'm from the English Department — Spruce, if you didn't catch my name before — and I know you're going to be majoring in Planning and Development, but you've simply got to take my Dickens Seminar. Of course, it's up to you to choose your own electives, but you would inspire that class with how you've connected on your own to these great works."

"Well, that sounds like fun. I don't get much chance to talk with others about Dickens in the course of my life up to now."

The Dean was grinning. "Dr. Spruce, I appreciate your enthusiasm, but we are getting a little ahead of ourselves here. We haven't awarded our scholarships yet."

"I can't help but get ahead of myself, your honor!" the man burst out in a new comical, joyous way that reminded Lawanda of a Dickens character. "This is a remarkable development — the kind that restores faith and propels one to new heights of hope! Reg, you won't regard it as poaching if I take a mere three hours per week of this prized student's time next semester?"

"'Course not — why are we always gassing about 'interdisciplinary studies' around here if we get all turf-protective the next minute. We could even do a couple of sessions together next fall, bringing our two classes together for 'Dickens and Urban Environments' — or something like."

"Great idea, all for it!" this English prof cried. "You see, Miss Tuffet, I grew up poor in the West Virginia mountains. I would have qualified myself for one of these need-based scholarships. Neither parent had a high school education. But like you, I read. When I could find anyone to talk to about it, I did that too, but mostly I read on my own and worked at figuring it out. Though it's often lied about, I know it can be done."

The Dean again had that big smile, looking back and forth at the two men. "Miss Tuffet, I think it's quite safe to say you will get our strong recommendation for this scholarship. The Committee is very likely to go along with that, though with academicians you can never be totally sure of anything. So, tentatively — congratulations!"

Lawanda started to tear up, but there was so much joy in the room, she got swept away into that. At one point this Professor Spruce of the English Department said something which she knew would stick in her head a long time: "You know it's such a freeing thing when you see you don't have everything figured out, and the universe really does offer surprises. We ought to be more open to that in academia. That anything really can happen."

The Dean was nodding yes to that.

Then Lawanda knew she would tell them. "You having made that point, I got to tell you all something that actually happened that I might not have believed until night before last. It was on an Amtrak overnight train coming down here to Florida. "My little fellow here wasn't sleeping well just leaning on my shoulder. He likes lying flat on a bed. He was whining on, and I couldn't quiet him down, and my neighbors in the coach were complaining because they couldn't sleep. Some were laying it on me pretty hard. It was going on four in the morning, and none of us passengers were happy campers.

"And then comes this hero savior into the coach. Someone I had never laid eyes on. It sounds like a fairy tale, but here was a ninety year old white man, having appeared out of nowhere, standing there in the aisle and offering to solve our problem. He took me back to his sleeper room and put me and my Shawn in his own bed. Can you believe that?"

"Really!" the Dean and Dr. Regnald said almost together.

"These things do happen," Dr. Spruce murmured.

"This Mr. Ted Costas told me that being old, he was an early riser and had already slept enough. That might be true, but I know he said it to make me more comfortable."

"Sounds like the kind of story in a Dickens novel that certain modernist and post-modernist intellectuals would absolutely despise," this Professor Spruce said.

"Truly? Why?"

"They would say because something like that wouldn't really happen, but I think the real reason is it doesn't fit the ironic worldview they depend on. If they took it seriously, it would scare them with new possibility. Maybe threaten to stir up old hopes, long buried in self protection."

"Well, I'll have to think about that."

"Once he had you and baby in his sleeper bed,"Dr. Regnand asked, "what did he do?"

"Well, he sat down beside me in the sleeper room on the little chair. He said it was so he could explain to the porter if he looked in on us. When I woke up, he took me and the boy to breakfast in the diner."

There was a silence in the room, and even though there was sunlight streaming in behind the Dean's desk, to Lawanda it now seemed to flush much brighter. Again, the flash of a strobe, illuminating not just the stories in this room but those of Granny T slowly losing her memory and of Devon, her own estranged "Pre-owned Vehicle Representative" wherever in Kentucky he was, those poor folks in the police station yesterday who were hoping to get Harley as their lawyer "who don't take nothing from no judge", and Mr. Ted Costas of Baltimore, Maryland wherever, dear soul, he might be at this very moment.

"Like you said sir," she sang out suddenly to Professor Spruce, "in that happening on the train, we see the beautiful freedom of the world, the shining city on the hill, where folks really can do wonders!"

Chapter Three:
What Legacy?

Solomon Junior's younger brother Luke was back in town, and there was nothing he could do about it. Mary Louise, sister of both, was actually excited by the news, but she knew that Sol Junior, being the cautious and conservative first child that he was, could only sustain limited exposure to Luke, being the comically wild and generally over-the-top kid brother that he was. Not to mention that said younger brother had now become an out-of-work philosopher. Mary Louise considered this a dangerous breed — especially to put around an old line family cleaning business, which the elder brother ran like it was some kind of national trust preservation property, for which any change might lead to de-certification and sudden death.

"So Luke went and got himself fired by that university in Ohio?" husband Britt asked her.

"Said he didn't get tenure. His carefully reasoned explanation I can just about quote you: 'That Retention Committee is wholly made up of obscurantist numbskulls whose sole occupation in life is to make certain that the language of academic philosophy remains so arcane that no outsiders could possibly understand or apply it to anything breathing.'"

"Umm. Sounds like Luke."

"Now he wants to be called by his real name," she told him. "Maybe he needs that, having been tossed from that university."

"What is it exactly?"

"'Lucilius.'"

"Umm. That's hard to remember."

It was a name that the invited guest, Fauna, also found hard to remember at that first Sunday dinner at Sol Junior's. Mary Louise had come up with that schedule for controlled exposure: younger brother Lucilius would join her, husband and twelve year old daughter for dinner at the pleasant house of the older brother most Sunday evenings, with the subtly communicated understanding that otherwise he would stay out of his hair. Why host Sol Junior had also invited Fauna — his long-time friend whom folks had first thought he might marry — remained unclear, though Mary Louise guessed she had been asked as a sort of wet blanket stranger for the Kid Brother, in a preemptive strike to damp him down.

"It's good to meet you, Lucilium," Fauna began, looking up at him earnestly. "Is that right – did I say it correctly?"

"Hardly. Madame, you have neutered me."

"What? I only —"

"The "u-m" you put at the end of my Latin name is reserved for nouns in the neuter. Your version would be appropriate for a species of bacterium, forever neuter and sexless."

"Oh, so sorry, I —"

"I may be many things, but not a bacterium. Nor a neuter of any species. I am a human male, with a Latin name shown as masculine by its second declension, "u-s" ending — ie., "Lucili*us*.!

"Now having got that totally clear..." Mary Louise intervened.

"Fauna, would you like a drink?" Sol Junior asked.

"For sure!" The woman was clearly rattled.

Unusual for her – what Solomon Jr. seemed to like was her ordinary placidity. She gave Younger Brother a wide berth, navigating around him toward a sofa in the living room where she could settle down into the bland and sedentary posture that was comfortable to her.

Luke — Mary Louise still called him that to herself — may have seen his effect on the guest Fauna, because he was unusually quiet for a time, allowing his older brother to launch into a reminiscence of earlier days at the cleaning business, this prompted by old newspaper clippings his secretary had discovered that day.

Solomon Junior became quite glowing over these memories of better times, with Fauna doing her usual workman-like job of seconding everything he said. This allowed Mary Louise to observe the Prodigal Younger Brother Returned, noting that though he appeared as wild-eyed and wild-haired as when she'd seen him at Christmas, he was wearing a nice-looking jacket and slacks — a possible concession to the hometown Parrot world to which he had returned? Of course, with his general unbuttoned style he could never match the proper respectability emanating from his older brother, Sol Junior, as he presided over this family dinner which he habitually purchased, all prepared, from the same local caterer. Despite the family name, this oldest surviving Parrot always shunned bright colors and more resembled an owl with his round tortoise shell spectacles, wide eyes and down-turned nose – which made him appear always to be looking down on something before him with reserved distaste.

"Those were great times," Sol Junior said now, concluding his nostalgic account of the family business. "I believe it's fair to say that for a period of at least twenty years there, Solomon Parrot, Cleaners and Menders, was the leading firm of its kind in the area. Dad left it at that high level, and I was able to keep it there for some years. But not now. We're not there anymore. That era is history." He shook his head slowly, staring down into the dregs of his drink.

"But still a good business, Solly," Fauna reassured him. "And very respected in the community."

"Yes, that is true."

"So what if other cleaners are more dominant now?" Mary Louise asked him. "If it brings in enough for your needs, what's the difference?" What she didn't say was *And you've got no wife or children but are a middle-aged bachelor who seems to get more fun out of saving money than spending it, so what's your problem?*

"It's like an empire," Solomon Jr. brooded gloomily. "If it's not expanding, it's contracting."

Luke looked up, suddenly interested. "Oh, I get it — you don't want to be remembered as an 'Emperor of the Decline and Fall.' No Nero you — in freshly dry-cleaned *toga* — fiddling while the Parrot Empire burns."

His solemn brother made a face, not buying in.

But that did lead to continuing discussion over dinner — memories of the lost days when Solomon Parrot had been the dominant cleaning company for miles around. Mary Louise could tell that her kid brother was starting to get interested philosophically in the question, always a dangerous sign.

"Listen," he broke in. "I think I've got it.

What Dad instigated — the genius of Solomon Senior in this — was jingles! You remember that? All over town people would recite those things."

Sol Junior shook his head. "That was his era. Jingles used to be big in advertising. Then they came to be considered corny and old-fashioned. We had to cut them out."

Luke looked off, in that sort of pregnant way, Mary Louise thought — you knew something big was growing inside him.

"People may grow tired of jingles or think them corny," he said, "yet those are but attitudes."

His older brother looked annoyed: "So what else would they—"

"Mere attitudes don't change the imprinting of the human brain. Rhymes are remembered. In philosophy, we call that a 'phenomenon'. However you try to *explain* it, a Phenomenologist would regard it as a starting point, a base datum. There's your neuter, Fauna — a datum, beyond gender or explanation."

"Aren't we getting a little far afield here?" Mary Louise put in.

"Not at all. Since a rhyme is encoded as a base phenomenon in the brain, a person may not like a rhyme, but still remembers it. That's why jingles will always work in advertising."

Solomon Junior continued to look owlishly discontent, but Fauna's face had opened into a child-like smile. "I remember one — can still say it:

If you rip it,
If you tear it,
Solomon Parrot
Will repair it!

"There you go!" Lucilius, Kid Brother Returned and Rejected Philosopher, settled back at the table with the greatest satisfaction.

It turned out they all did remember that, and could recite it with pleasure. Even young daughter Nina, who had never heard it before, was enchanted and quickly committed it to memory. Luke was validated and beamed benignly on all. For the moment, Mary Louise thought, a true Philosopher King.

"There were others jingles that Sol Senior put in," Luke added. "One was based on a nursery rhyme — though I can't quite remember it."

"I thought rhymes were 'base phenomena of the human brain' which one couldn't forget", Mary Louise chided him.

For only a moment did the Philosopher King seem in danger of being pulled from the throne. "Difference between long and short term memory,

M.L. In short term, you will remember a rhyming thing almost perfect, line for line. And that is what matters for advertising. In long term — with no reinforcement over years — you may forget lines. But notice: I did remember *the fact of it*, the existential reality and impact of that rhyming jingle."

At that, the whole company went to work on bits and pieces. They all agreed that there had been several other jingles to the eternal glory of Solomon Parrot, Cleaners and Menders, though they couldn't recall more than a couple of rhyming lines here and there.

"You see," Luke broke in, "this is fun for all!

Despite the frustration of not remembering key lines, we're all pursuing these rhymes like gold at the end of the rainbow. There's your phenomenon imprinted in the cerebral hemisphere!"

Given the cautious excitement now shown even by the normally depressed Solomon Junior and the placidly conventional Fauna, Mary Louise could see that Lucilius the Great was sweeping all before him, and she wondered where it would end.

By the desert course, which she brought in from the refrigerator to help out, this began to come clearer. After one taste of the Lemon Meringue, Luke stood abruptly at the end of the table, holding the sticky pie fork aloft as a sort of talisman of his new power, and addressed the company: "Bro Sol, I aim to restore this empire!"

Mary Louise noted her two contrasting reactions: that her worst fears had been realized and that this might be a lot of fun.

"All too clear that there is a regrettable absence of philosophy in fabrics enhancement as practiced at Solomon Parrot Incorporated," Luke pursued. "To begin, it is too often assumed that customer and management agree on what constitutes enhancement. But what would be the shared epistemological basis there? I will remedy that lack and draw as well on the rhyme addiction of the human brain by applying the lessons of Phenomenology. And you will observe the result: men and women will be *deeply drawn* to bring us their dirty sheets and soiled underclothes, sweaty cummerbunds and bloated bolsters – not knowing why perhaps but perceiving, if only in their dim unconscious, the advantage of having their cleaning and mending done by a firm grounded in sound epistemological and rhetorical principles! Our competitors will be left in shambles."

Sol Junior wore a curious look of fascination drenched in horror.

"But for that to happen, Bro Sol, you must appoint me to a new corporate office: 'Phenomenological Potentate for Jingles'. For the company, this will be a no-risk proposition. For my remuneration, I ask a mere percentage of the increase in net receipts. I believe one half of that net increase per month — each month, that is, from the original base of the present — would be equitable."

"Now just a doggone minute!" Sol Junior rallied.

"Let's hear more of what he has in mind," Mary Louise weighed in. After all, she still owned a share of this family business.

"Thank you, Madam, for your intellectual progressivism! My first act as P.P.J. would be to restore that famous jingle close to many hearts still beating in our town, I'm sure — and linked to the glorious empire founded by Solomon Senior himself. Then I will begin to research the lost jingles — that we might restore them too to their rightful rhetorical roles."

"You said you want fifty percent of the *net* increase?" Sol Jr. asked.

"Correct."

"That means if you overspend our ad budget on this, you'll get little or nothing."

"I am fully aware of that limitation."

That may have been true, Mary Louise reflected, but in general there didn't seem to be many limitations that Luke was aware of. During the next week he became a continual persistent presence at Parrot headquarters. Sol Junior's secretary, Mudge, who had discovered the cache of old company files that had led to her boss's nostalgia, could hardly attend to her normal duties for Luke's one man archaeological expedition into the "old files" in her office. "That man is obsessed!" she told Mary Louise during the week.

"Yes, whenever he gets a philosophical bit between his teeth...that tends to happen." But at least he had something to become obsessed about, Mary Louise told herself. She, by contrast, had become such a drifter at forty — depending on her husband's job for all her material sustenance and on her shadow life as a volunteer among old people — who hardly recognized anything, much less herself in her efforts at sustaining them. She had never stood out like her kid brother with his restless energy and wild-haired look, but now more than ever she seemed to be settling in as a simple faced woman in plain clothes, hard to remember outside the family. What impact did she have on any one?

By contast, the fired-up brother phoned her the next day, breathless: "I've found him!"

"Found who?"

"The genius who understood that jingles would set this company on a higher plane, way above its competitors. Vaguely remembered that Sol Senior contracted with a lone wolf advertising man to create those jingles."

"You mean all came from the same —"

"Correct. From 'Theodore Costas, Product Promotion'. That was the name of his one-man operation in Baltimore. Never came out here to see what he had done for the Parrot Empire — anyway, not that I can find."

The reason Luke was so excited, he explained to her, was that now he knew where to look for the other jingles. "Once found," he explained, "they will extend the hold of the Parrot Empire on the hidden mimetic systems of the unsuspecting populace."

"You couldn't find them in those files you've been pouring through for three days?"

"Not a one. What I think is that Sol Junior made some brash judgment that they were all old hat and tossed them."

"Umm. Refreshing though to think of him as doing something brash."

"Interesting point." Luke sucked in his lips and looked at her. "M.L., despite our different styles, I must say you are the one who has a good take on what's going down here in the old home town, around the old Parrot Empire. And with a feel for its current-day *Weltanschauung*. I give you credit."

Mary Louise was touched. She'd often thought that there was some area of emotional understanding where this so intellectual and ironic younger brother did value her, and now he had gone and said it. "Thank you, Dr. Lucilius. The world is a mysterious place, but I try."

"Yes. And what is your take on that Fauna person? What is her role in the world of Sol Jr?"

"Not his girlfriend or future wife, though the aunts at first were all sure of that. Something like 'Companion to Keep His Spirits Up.'"

"And reassure him of his importance?"

"Right. But she's available if you're looking for a female companion to calm you down and keep you on an even keel."

"You taunt me. Immortal Gods — if I took her on, I would become too calmed down for any actual respiration to occur!"

Mary Louise had to laugh. He was in effect vice president of a company, at least for the moment, but he would never learn to do public relations corporate talk, and his rebellious hair alone would cause scandal at the Chamber of Commerce. "Fauna aside," she told him, "I know you've got no time for romance, being too hot on the heels of this Jingle Genius you've uncovered. And I have to agree that he did put us on the map with lines like "Solomon Parrot, Immaculate Cleaner for a Dingy World".

"That's it — another bit you remembered! I know Ted Costas created not only jingles but slogans like that for us. Consider the literary satire in that phrase, 'immaculate cleaner for a dingy world'. As if anyone could be that — the man subtly mocks grandiose ambition. What a genius!"

She saw his point but was more impressed with the effect on business. On the first of May the company's local radio commercials had switched from boring straight announcements to the classic jingle they had all remembered, and by June 1 net receipts had climbed fifteen percent.

"Now, speaking as a Phenomenologist, I ask you to observe this deep effect on the human psyche," Luke told them at Sunday dinner that week. "It is rhyming repetition and clever ironic phrasing which draws them like lemmings."

"Could just be the novelty," Fauna — nasally from the couch.

"Or nostalgia," Sol Junior added. "This man's jingles and slogans remind lots of older folks around here of their childhood."

"If either of those is the explanation, the added business will go away quickly," Mary Louise said. "But you know what a couple of the old ladies did at Heavenly Rest when I was there Wednesday volunteering? They had been waiting for me, and they sort of drew themselves up and warbled out the "repair it" jingle.

"Not surprised in the least," Luke said.

Meantime, Sol Junior looked impressed in spite of himself.

"But I keep trying to remember the slogan Mr. Costas created to follow that," Luke went on. "It was similar to 'Immaculate Cleaner for a Dingy World', but not a cleaning slogan like that but a repair slogan. Just can't recall it."

"Still going to Baltimore next week to see if you can get some of those forgotten ones straight from the horse's mouth?" Mary Louise asked.

"That horse might have left the barn," Sol Jr. said. "Being Dad's generation, he might by now have wandered out into the great pasture in the sky."

Luke shook his own mane of wild and curly brown hair. "Thought of that, bro. But I found a current address for him in the online phone book. Thought about calling him, but decided in person would be better. Harder for him to brush me off, plus I'm curious to meet him."

That was intriguing enough that two days later Mary Louise was eagerly awaiting his return from Baltimore. To a degree that surprised her, these old jingles and slogans from the family business — remembered or half-remembered — promised to bring with them lost memories from her girlhood, which she felt a need for these days. Her husband Britt was a good man who kept her grounded, but he was not one for reflection and did not seem to share her sense that certain past life experiences needed recalling for present use. She left a message on Luke's cell phone to please drop by for a late breakfast his first day back.

"Good news and bad news," he began, as soon as he had his muffin and coffee set before him. "Which you want first?"

She settled opposite him at the kitchen table. "I always prefer to get the bad news out of the way."

"All right. This Mr. Ted Costas has died. Only a little over two months ago. He was ninety. The further bad news is that he hardly left any survivors. A tenant at his old apartment building gave me the phone number of the woman who had been married to his nephew, also deceased. She seems to be a harsh and stupid woman who has nothing of interest to say about him. Three days after his death she arranged for a used furniture company to come to his apartment and clear out everything for a set price. Didn't even bother going though his drawers or an old trunk first — that's how much she cared about him."

"I'm sorry he's died before you could talk to him. I mean, assuming he was still coherent?"

"Oh, very much so, from what I heard. In a somewhat altered state, it sounds like, but quite lucid."

"So what's the good news?"

"What I said: that harsh widow of his nephew didn't bother going though his stuff first before letting the furniture guy take it away."

"I don't—"

"Because if she had, she would likely have just tossed it all. Would have been nothing of value to her. Since she didn't bother, I was able to track the lot down to the used furniture warehouse, where they hadn't processed it yet. The owner let me pack his papers in boxes and take them away."

"So what did you find?"

"None of our jingles. And none of the accompanying slogans. And nothing like that for any of his other clients either. Quite strange I thought — that was his life's work, and he doesn't seem to have kept a piece of it."

"So when does the good news start?"

"Among his papers I did find references to his best remaining friend. These two old guys used to go out and eat at a local bar every week. I went to the address listed there and found only his daughter, because he — Mr. Ted's buddy — had died too, just this January. But the daughter had known and loved Ted Costas, and so I offered her the boxes of his stuff — which she gladly accepted, and I brought them up from my car trunk. She was about to leave her house for some appointment, so I just mentioned briefly that I was there looking for his jingles for Solomon Parrot Cleaners. And practically out the door, she quoted me one of ours — the only one she knew. Didn't even have to write it down, because I knew I would remember."

Luke sat back, took a sip of coffee and ran his hand though the wildly wiry atop his head, as though to smooth it. As usual, it was not calmed and sprang back, bristling with the same energy. "She had found it among the things her dad had left behind, and it had stuck in her head. Turned out to be the actual jingle that preceded that slogan you remembered. So the whole thing would have gone like this:

> If your clothes are twenty carat,
> But badly soiled by your pet ferret,
> Or slopped all over by peas and carrot,
> Or worn by an artist in a grubby garret,
> Bring one and all to Solomon Parrot!

> — Solomon Parrot,
> Immaculate Cleaner for a Dingy World.

"Wow," Mary Louise said. "That brings it back."

"How you mean?"

"From when I was a little girl. I remember that I wanted to know from that jingle what was an 'artist in a grubby garret?' I asked mom and got some stuff to read on it and got very excited about the whole idea of such an artist. The bohemian life, painting nudes in one's studio — all that. So you know what I did — it's so funny now! I went to the studio of the only artist I knew about — Jenny McTee."

Luke had broken out his grin: "Portraitest of demure children, Jenny McTee. Middle aged maiden lady. Assume you didn't find much of the bohemian life there."

"Well, she was the only artist in town that this little girl had ever heard about. I figured an artist was an artist!"

"Kid's thinking make as much sense as any."

"So instead of nudes with violins sitting for her drawings, I found only little girls in prim lace collars, squirming in their chairs and asking for another piece of candy."

"What I love about reality," Luke enthused. "If you're paying attention, it's so rarely what you expect."

He cleared his throat and looked more serious. "But there's more info. As I told you, Ted Costas was much liked by his buddy's daughter, Carol. Though I only saw her for a minute that night, we exchanged email addresses — I thought I might have follow-up questions for her. Surprised me when I got home and found her message, giving me some touching history on the man. Decades ago, when he and his wife were middle-aged, their two children—the girl home from college, the boy a senior in high school—were killed when a drunk driver smashed into their car as they were driving back late from a Christmas party. She said

Ted Costas never got over that and was looking for substitute children to give to all his life."

"Mmmn. So you start off looking for old advertising jingles, and you come up with the tragedy of life."

"And strangely enough, that ties right back into the jingles. According to Carol's email, when his children were killed, Mr. Ted Costas was a small time advertising man, but he had never written any rhyming copy. She wrote that it was in the year following his kids' death that he "found rhyming" — her way of putting it. He had told her that the rhyming gave him both a discipline and 'some reassuring thing' he needed. Told her that it gave him a sense of everything being connected and the world being more than just random craziness. So it 'sort of kept me on the rails, instead of running into a ditch'. That was how he put it to her."

"And then that became his meal ticket — and I guess his legacy."

"For us, at least. It sure put Solomon Parrot on the map, and Ted Costas was brilliant at it, knowing how to create what would stick in human memories. But that's not all."

"Meaning what?"

"In the email Carol actually used that word 'legacy' as well. But she said he seemed to think that his legacy was working with kids and teenagers. Tutoring those who were not doing well."

"Something apart from his vaunted jingle-making."

Luke shook that off. "Maybe not. Because she wrote that he did creative stuff with the kids using rhymes — to get them paying attention to words."

Mary Louise poured herself a second cup of coffee and stared over her brother's shoulder into the backyard of their new house, which now suddenly reminded her of the backyard of her childhood. "Well, if we imitate Mr. Costas, you and I will live almost another fifty years, but suppose we die tomorrow. What would people say we were all about? What would they name as our legacies, yours and mine?"

"Hate to think of the labels they would stick on us!"

"I hope they'd hesitate and feel their way there, with a proper sense of mystery."

"You're an optimist, M.L. Most prefer clear definition to mystery."

"Probably. They'd likely say you were a philosopher and wanted to bring out how complicated and profound everything was."

"And the truth is the opposite — I want to sweep away excess verbiage and muddled thinking, going for as much clarity as possible!" He gave her an intimate little smile, not his usual look at all: " And you. What would they say in your obituary? Maybe something like, "Out of her great compassion, she tended our oldest citizens in their pain and loss of faculties." ·

"And as with you, mostly the opposite is true: I don't do it out of compassion as much as out of interest. I find the very old are interesting to attend because they've often lost manners and pretense — making them like children, but with experience. So you can see bare humanity there: plenty mean and selfish but also at times getting over themselves to something better. The whole human package comes clearer."

"Very good, M.L. So — judging from us — you think all true legacies, like life, will remain unclear and shrouded in mystery?"

"I think so. But it seems the genius of Mr. Costas at rhyme and phrase making — that maybe gave him his legacy of tutoring students, and did become a major force in creating the Parrot Empire, as you've been calling it — all that has changed lives."

"And will again! I'm adding that jingle Carol told me in Baltimore to our radio and TV ads. I'm telling you: this Empire will rise from the ashes of Solomon Junior's defeatism and depression. On the strength of mimetic harmonies imprinted on human cerebella, it will rise again!"

He added the cleaning jingle of ferrets and garrets to radio and TV spots that week, and even put one on a billboard near Parrot headquarters.

What happened next caused no one in the family to doubt that the monthly net receipts would show another major jump: people began to call the office. They wanted to be reminded how a line went, they wanted to say how much fun they thought the jingles were, they wanted to share jingle lines they had just composed — sometimes for a fee, but sometimes offered free to the company in the joy of authorship. Some just wished to share associations from childhood stirred up by the words so long forgotten.

One afternoon Mary Louise happened to be with Sol Jr. in his office when she heard a commotion in the reception area without, the door banging open and someone storming in.

"What's that!" — Sol Jr., alarmed.

"MUDGE!" — a voice in the outer office — "you can forget pawing through old file cabinets on your knees and rise again from that rear-first posture!"

They rushed to the reception area and saw Sol Jr.'s motherly secretary — on the floor next to a bottom drawer — now falling back awkwardly in the wake of the charging Luke.

"What is this about?" Sol Jr — stolidly attempting calm.

"Bro Sol, it has hit me. Took two days of our customers calling about the jingles for the implications to penetrate my thick cranium!"

"Come on, Luke," Mary Louise said. "Tell us already."

"Get Mudge up off the floor — we don't need to keep researching this. Our customers will do it for us!"

"They'll research what?"

"What Mr. Ted Costas, Genius Jinglist and Phrase-Maker, bequeathed us. Make it a public contest — reward the first person to deliver each lost jingle or slogan! We'll get 'em all inside a month."

Sol Jr. stroked his chin but looked interested.

"And you see how much better that is? Then the public is invested in this. It's *their* jingles too!"

"That's pretty smart, Luke," Mary Louise commented. "Maybe Philosophy and Commerce can be friends."

"Thanks, M.L. Do you hear it — that rumbling, ripping sound? It's the roar of a rising empire, having subsided into the mud, but now breaking through the surface crust, rising on the back of sound phenomenological rhetoric — like some horny-plated behemoth of ancient times!"

Not such an exaggeration, Mary Louise thought, based on the response to the contest. This wild philosophical kid brother of theirs was proving out as a business man — even to his suggestion that they'd better make clear that no contest entries would be accepted by phone, or Mudge would have little time for anything else.

It was truly astonishing how the efforts at resurrected jingles and slogans flooded in by postman and email, even though the prize for the first correct version of each was only ten dollars off a cleaning bill. As the kid brother, Dr. Lucilius, put it, "To these folks, this means a lot more than money."

Luke even anticipated that some of the jingles received would be "new artistic efforts, no matter what we say", and advised that the best of these should be acknowledged to the creators and put in a separate file for possible future adoption. At the end of the month, business was up eighty-eight percent from the pre-Lukean era.

"You're looking like the proverbial canary-devouring cat," Mary Louise told him at the next Sunday dinner, while Sol Jr. was still upstairs.

"Well, I'm moving into a better apartment for one thing," he told her.

"That's how sure you are that your earnings based on the business's net increase are no short-term blip?"

"That plus I interviewed out at the community college for an opening in Philosophy in the fall. I think I'm going to get it."

Mary Louise thought her face must have shown surprise.

"It might just suit me. It's temporary for this year, but they expect to add a permanent position for next. And they don't tenure people based on abstruse research which no one but other philosophy professors can even understand, much less care about. The Dean there told me they want 'someone who can make philosophical questions real, and so enrich the outlook of our students.' I tend to believe him."

"Well, well. I can see you fitting into that."

"In the interest of full disclosure, it didn't hurt that I met a couple of cute female professors."

"Aha."

Mary Louise was quiet, stirred by all this and not knowing how much to say. This was not something she would want to express in front of Sol Jr., after he came downstairs, and certainly not in front of husband Britt, who was scheduled to arrive a little later in a separate car. So time being limited, she decided to go straight at it: "I'm glad for you and — honestly — envious."

He was watching her with mild surprise: she was not given to such confessions. "You remember I told you about that jingle reminding me of my young girl visit to Jenny McTee's studio in hopes of discovering the Bohemian artist life?"

"That was funny."

"And sad. Undeterred by the absence of the Bohemian, I went back there a few times, seeing if I could learn from her how to draw. I was hopeless. Always have been in things artistic."

Now he looked a bit embarrassed for her, she thought.

"You know it's a mixed blessing Britt making so much that I've never had to work. It's given me a lot of time to question my value in the world. No, let me finish this, before anyone comes in. Our talk about that old man's legacy has brought this up stronger just now. Another cause is my getting ready for my Nina's return from summer camp at the end of the week. Right now she's at that early adolescent stage of questioning who *she* is going to be in the world. And — though she would never admit it in a million years — looking to her mom for some ideas. I'm very sensitive to that in her presence."

"Hmmn. Somewhat daunting aspect of having a kid. I've never had to think of that."

"Right, and I can't avoid thinking of it now. It's what I meant about envious as well as glad for you. I can see you making a contribution there at the community college, but it raises again: 'What is *my* contribution?'"

"I thought you valued your work at the old persons' home."

"As I said, old people are often interesting to me. But I don't know how much I help them. They usually don't remember what I say, and some don't even remember who I am from one day to another."

"Mmm. I see that."

"It's like working in a great fog of lost memories, in which all personalities, not to mention legacies, are lost forever."

The Kid Brother was watching her with more care in his face than she remembered seeing.

"Sometimes it seems that great fog is pouring out into my whole world, and I will be lost in it forever."

The front door was heard to open and Britt to call out heartily, but before he could enter the room and find them, Luke took time to quickly say, "Believe me, M.L., even in my most positivistic moods, I'm aware of that threat — the fog that swallows us."

She was always glad that he had given her that perspective on himself, because it seemed from that moment that everything related to Solomon Parrot Inc. marched into double-time, like speeded-up film in an old movie comedy. The company did indeed seem to be rising again as an empire based on slogans and jingles rediscovered by a town suddenly enchanted by its memories of the same — and gladly distracted by those rhythms from the boredom and anxieties of everyday life.

More evidence came before dinner as Luke began to share the slogans and jingles sent in by local citizens in the "Parrot Legacy Contest".

"First, folks, a Mrs. Minnie Ludwitz of Futzmiller Township wins a Clean and Mean Certificate for recalling the slogan that went with the classic "If you rip it, if you tear it" jingle. Ready? The paired slogan was (Tarrah!) "Solomon Parrot — Making Whole a World in Tatters.""

A delighted showing of smiles — even Britt seemed charmed by that one, Mary Louise thought.

"That Ted Costas," Luke exclaimed. "The man was a great ironist."

Sol Jr. was heard to answer Fauna's puzzled mumble with the quiet aside, "No, dear — nothing to do with the tool used in garment pressing. He means the man was sort of joking in the slogan that our company could repair the world."

But that wasn't all, Luke continued. An old man in the East End had become so excited he actually got out of his nursing home bed and had to be restrained when he remembered the jingle and closing slogan:

> *Soiled jeans of farmer-gleaners?*
> *Jacket spotted by big baked beaners?*
> *Dress shirt spattered from mustard wieners?*
> *Bring one and all to Parrot cleaners.*
>
> *~~Solomon Parrot. Cleaning Away the*
> *Debris of the Universe.*

As Potentate for Jingles, Luke added that one to the radio spots for the next week and appended the rediscovered "Making Whole a World in Tatters" slogan to the classic "Repair it" jingle.

But even Luke was likely not prepared for the television channel from a nearby city calling. They wanted to run a story on the "Parrot Legacy Contest" and what it was meaning to the town.

"Now that," proclaimed Solomon Junior, "— that is publicity you cannot buy with dollars."

It was the day after that special story ran on local television news that Luke asked Mary Louise to accompany him to Sol Jr.'s office, where he was going to propose something big. "It's going to take this to a whole higher plane," he told her.

In the inner office, Luke asked his two siblings to sit, though it seemed he himself surged with too much excitement for anything but a standing and pacing position. "Now you both know we've discussed expanding into West Drigsby," he began. "I still believe that's a natural new location for us. But as Thought should normally precede Action, something else must come first. We must first cement our standing as local legend."

"And how do we do that?" his big brother asked.

"Actually with cement. Partly. In fact, that will only form the pediment, the base of the thing."

"Of ... 'the thing'?"

"A statue on the company's front lawn. That scruffy yard will become a landscaped plaza, appropriate setting for a bronze memorial — the full figure with one hand holding a pen, the other a jotting pad to suggest inspiration coming to him in the moment."

"What full figure — of who?"

"*Theodore Costas. Jinglist and Poet.* Inscribed beneath."

Sol Jr. stared in silence, then began slowly but decisively wagging back and forth his head. "That's going too far. In fact, it's outlandish."

"So?" said Luke. "What has being 'landish' ever done for you?"

Sol Jr. quit wagging his head, though he continued to stare.

"Customers dropping off or picking up clothes at the side entrance will come around to see it. They'll tell out of town visitors the story and bring them to see it. They'll point it out to their kids and get them to read it, because of course we'll have all the jingles and slogans carved on plaques around the statue."

"Sort of like the Gettysburg Address in the Lincoln Memorial?" Mary Louise asked innocently.

"Ha, ha — good one, M.L. A thin line often between the comic and the sublime, but no matter. This is not supposed to be dead serious. Ted Costas didn't mean the ads to be."

"Too outlandish," Sol Jr repeated with that stunned expression.

At that Mary Louise jumped in: "How *outlandish* is it that net profits are up 104 percent in three months! That's *another land* from any this business has ever been in — right?"

"I suppose that's true. And I — we all, the family — are certainly grateful, Lucilius, for what you've accomplished here. But you must know we have no money for this."

"Thought about that, bro. It happens that an acquaintance of mine was also refused tenure this year and left that University. He happens to be a sculptor. A very much out-of-work sculptor with this recession being what it is. We've held talks, and he's intrigued by the project. And at least as intrigued by the dollar intake. He will do it at a price we can afford."

"Are you sure. I mean what kind of price—"

"I'm willing to donate half of my take from the business next month. You match that amount from your take, and withdraw another couple of thousand from reserves for his materials – all deductible as an advertising expense – and that will work for him."

While his older brother was hesitating, Luke unrolled a preliminary sketch showing everything — statue and plaques.

It looked good. Mary Louise could see that her older brother was warming to it, and that her younger one turned quite happy from this. She liked it too — there was a kind of gentle humor in the bronze face of "Theodore Costas, Jinglist and Poet" as he was taken by inspiration. In the conception he didn't look too grand or earnest. Mudge was called in, and she went for it as well. Not great art probably — though Mary Louise considered herself no judge of that — but there was nothing not to like.

"Suppose we decide to go ahead" – Sol Jr., very serious. "When could your sculptor and ex- professor start?"

"How about day after tomorrow?' Luke said.

Turned out it was all set up, just awaiting the approval Luke had expected. So on the same day she, Britt and Nina were scheduled to leave on their month-long family vacation, the sculptor — identified by Luke simply as "Bridges" — was to move into the second bedroom in his new apartment and begin working on the sculpture in a spare room in the cleaning plant.

"We'll schedule the public dedication and unveiling for Labor Day — a great day in the history of this town! You'll be back by then of course," he asked her.

"Of course," Mary Louise said. "But I'm surprised that he could do something like that, with the casting and everything in four weeks."

Luke looked just slightly embarrassed. "Well, let's just say he's had a bit of a head start."

Britt's brother had a place on a Lake in Maine, and that's where they were headed again to cool off and get away, as on the two summers before. Two girl cousins of about her same age would be there for Nina. She loved being with them, and Mary Louise felt relieved as well that for a few weeks she wouldn't have to be the only adult female model for her daughter. The cousins' mother was an attractive woman, with a certain kind of confidence that Mary Louise felt she lacked.

As usual, they all enjoyed the lake — the kids swimming and kayaking, the men fishing and drinking, and the women talking, walking and kayaking. As a couple, she and Britt went off on moose-photographing expeditions. He always wanted her to drive while he got out of the car to take pictures. Not an entirely safe thing to be doing, but she was glad for Nina to see them cooperating in something adventurous together.

Luke kept everyone informed by email of speedy progress on "the memorial". And he described how two old brothers living near the cleaning plant had submitted a perfect version of the nursery rhyme jingle which Luke had been unable to recall. They had won the "Clean and Mean Certificate" for the week and been interviewed on local television as to their history with the jingle and how they had remembered it — ending with a spirited recitation. "Just imagine this, folks," Luke wrote, "by two old guys singing in barber shop quartet style, and sounding great!

One Two, buckle my shoe.
Three four, coat on the floor,
Five six, coat in a ditch,
Seven eight, we press it straight.
Nine ten, we give it a mend.
Eleven twelve, our cleaners delve
Thirteen fourteen, it's ready for sportin'!

Trust your outsides to us.
We'll cover for you. ~~ Solomon Parrot

Meanwhile up at the lake, the three young girls got up their own performance of this latest jingle, adding syncopated dance movements, out on the deck one night. Some neighbors with kids had been invited in, and it was greeted with great applause.

As September approached, Luke's emails became less frequent, as he was preparing his new classes at the community college, but he wrote that he had hired a couple of local kids to help Bridges with some of the physical stuff as they approached the casting, and later the sinking of the bronze statue into its concrete base and the attaching of the written tablets to the brick wall behind.

As the day to leave Maine neared, Mary Louise found she was quite ready. Her mind kept trying to picture the Ted Costas Memorial and its unveiling ceremony. "Let's not stop but drive straight through," she urged. "That way we'll get home with a little to spare before Labor Day."

They agreed to do that, and the family van arrived in town late Saturday night. The next morning they were all too tired for church, but around noon she phoned Luke.

To her enthusiastic question of whether everything was ready for the big day tomorrow, she got a low-voiced, muffled response she couldn't hear.

"What's wrong — you anxious about some things still not in place?"

"Oh, no. Everything is terribly well in place. Terribly complete."

"Luke, what is it?"

"Not on the phone. Could you come over here? Bridges is out, so we could speak privately."

"I'll be there in half an hour."

When he opened the door to his new apartment — which he had showed off to her with enthusiasm just before she left for Maine — he looked pale and depressed, like she'd never seen him. What could this *be*?

"Do you remember who Carol is?" he asked quickly, as though he wanted to get through this fast, couldn't bear not to.

"Isn't that the daughter of Ted Costas's old man buddy, whom you told me about?"

"Right. You remember she recited me one of his jingles she happened to remember just as I was leaving, having dropped off his stuff. And then she emailed me something about his life."

"I do recall that now — about the death of his own kids and how that affected him."

He nodded, not looking her in the face.

"I phoned her this morning to invite her to the memorial dedication tomorrow. Told her what a big deal it was going to be, apologized for forgetting to invite her sooner. Knowing how she felt about him, I was sure she would want to come."

"Yes, and…"

"She told me definitively that he wouldn't have come himself. She knows him far better than any of us, and she said if there were such a thing as ghosts, his would haunt that memorial to scare away visitors."

"Whatever for!"

"She told me he hated remembering that part of his life. Regarded his advertising work as lies. Said that whenever it was mentioned, he would shake his head disgustedly, and say the best thing about retiring and getting old was that now he "had no time for anything but the truth."

"But didn't she write you something to the effect that discovering his rhyming ability helped to steady him at the time his children were killed, 'kept him on the rails', or some such?"

"The rhyming itself was a gift he was glad to have discovered. What disgusted him was the use he then put it to in advertising jingles, the lies they often told."

"Oh. I see."

"So we have a quite clear statement of his feelings about all this. Perfectly understandable. Admirable even. But pretty awful now to someone who just blundered ahead, never considering that his life's work — which so benefited *us* and seemed so droll — might have meant something very different to him."

After a long pause, Mary Louise said quietly, "Well, that does now make sense of some other things. Like why you couldn't find any slogans or jingles in those old drawers of his."

He nodded in a way that indicated he'd thought of that. "You can imagine how I now feel about tomorrow, though I know we have to go through with it."

Mary Louise decided to make her best stab at comfort: "After all, he's dead and gone. And whatever he would feel about that part of his life, it's a very positive legacy for the townspeople here — and obviously our company. What do they say, 'The world belongs to the living'? But I understand it hurts. You want to be honoring *him* and now… I feel the pain of that too."

"I don't really want to talk about it. Maybe later. We have to get through tomorrow with smiles on. I just ask one thing."

"Yeah?"

"That at tomorrow's ceremonies, on the so- called 'Dignitaries Platform' where I have to be placed and keep up a happy face, will you please sit next to me?"

The ceremonies were to begin at noon. Mary Louise nosed her car in beside Sol Jr.'s in the parking spaces reserved for dignitaries behind the company building. She was there early, as planned. Britt and Nina were to come later in the other car and sit in the audience chairs out front. She went to meet Luke in Mudge's office and found him in conversation with the event planner, those who were to speak and other special guests.

When he was done with them, he ducked away and took her arm. "Let's get out of here and seated, before I have to talk more. This is going to be so much ado — so much of it about nothing. Nothing true, that is."

"Much of it is true to these people. It's a beautiful Labor Day, and they're very glad to be here for something that's a part of their memories, their history, their town."

"Okay, okay." Luke paused. "Actually, I don't mind your saying that kind of thing — even if it sugar coats. Maybe I do need to credit it some."

Before noon, the folding chairs were full and people were standing behind. Across the street, some had thrown out picnic blankets on the little hill of the cemetery, to watch from that higher view. There were flags and red, white and blue bunting, and a band began playing. Mary Louise thought *As far as possible I'm not going to think about what Mr. Ted Costas's reaction would be. Instead, I will try to appreciate how to those watching this is a special day of remembrance and a festive rest from their labors.*

Off to the side of the platform where she sat with the other "dignitaries", were great mounds of tarp covering the statue and the tablets inscribed with Mr. Costas's slogans and jingles written for the company. Before them, where the audience sat in folding chairs, the ground had been attractively paved in soft earth colors and landscaped where there was a natural rise.

A large bronze sign had been implanted: "Parrot Plaza".

"This whole place looks tons better than it ever has," she whispered to Luke, while Sol Jr. was solemnly reading to the audience a list of all the company employees who had died since the founding of the company by his father, "who I am sure are here with us in spirit on this day."

"Much ado, much ado." Luke whispered back in that despairing way.

Following, the remarks of Sol Jr. as Parrot President, the mayor stood to read a proclamation thanking Solomon Parrot Inc. for developing the plaza "to memorialize a piece of our local commercial history" and allowed that he wouldn't be surprised if this became a tourist attraction for the area, which would help many a town business.

"I gave him that," Luke whispered. "All the blood is on my hands."

Following the mayor, a news person from the nearby television channel which had sponsored the interviews of the Parrot Legacy Contest winners introduced them all — to an instant band salute and sustained applause. Each, including the two old brothers in barbershop close harmony, chanted into the microphone the jingle and slogan they had recovered, to loud cheering and the delight of all.

Next, following a drum roll, came the dramatic unveiling of the statue itself and the flanking inscribed tablets. The audience stood and cheered, while across the street those in the cemetery rose from among the stones of the dead, shouting and waving picnic napkins in the air.

Sol Jr. concluded the affair by reading a sort of combined history and encomium of "the life of this great Jinglist and Poet, and his contribution to commercial culture in general and to our town in particular. Collectively, we thank him," he proclaimed. "We bless him for bestowing his gift on us. What a legacy he has left!"

The band broke into celebratory sound. There was a great deal of happy milling about and congratulating of the dignitaries afterwards, and Luke grinned gamely and muttered thanks through many handshakes.

But suddenly he was staring over the heads of well-wishers: "Whoa!"

Mary Louise had remained resolutely at his side, as he had asked. "What *is* it?"

He didn't answer but seized her hand and began pushing his way through the crowd, pulling her along.

He stopped where a trim, fifty-something woman stood reading the jingles and slogans off the bronze tablets. "You came," he said to her.

"Couldn't stay away," she said. "I loved that man."

"This is Carol, the daughter of Mr. Ted's buddy, who also died this year. My sister, Mary Louise Botts."

"I thought it must be you," Mary Louise said, looking into the woman's frank, kind face. "Judging from Luke's excitement."

"This is quite a presentation of his advertising talent," Carol commented, indicating all the tablets. Mary Louise was struck by the woman's air of quiet competance, as though she had nothing to prove but was ready for anything. Even her wine-colored blouse and culottes skirt managed to look individual, effortless and yet attractive.

"What you explained about Mr. Costas's bad memories of his advertising career — no one else here knows that, but it's had quite an impact on Luke and me."

The woman was silently nodding, looking at the ground, reflecting. "Let me clarify something there. I never remember him saying anything bad — or anything at all — about the jingles he wrote for Solomon Parrot, Inc. It's true that he carried with him a bitterness about having wasted his talent with words on commercial advertising, and there's no getting around that. But I know the worst for him was something else – that he had been a wordsmith for a handful of big national corporations which he distrusted. He thought they were misleading and exploiting the public, but he couldn't make a living without their contracts. And that wasn't about your company."

"Well, that is something," Luke said.

"And I'm glad I came to this," Carol added. "The townspeople's response to the jingles and other bits he wrote — there was something playful, even joyous, in that which I wouldn't have guessed. In that they did get some flavor of the man, Ted's own style in writing them."

Mary Louise jumped at that: "Luke, you know how you were talking about Mr. Costas being 'a great ironist' and maybe skeptic philosopher — some such you said? In his writing slogans like *Solomon Parrot — Making whole a world in tatters?* I agree with her: I think this audience — and people generally — get the comic mockery of our human pretensions there. "

Luke was beginning to look more normal, even his hair seemed to be springing back the wrong way again. "Good, M.L. Good, Carol. Or take *Solomon Parrot — immaculate cleaner to a dingy world,* for instance. You're saying the delightful comic grandiosity of that comes through to most folks, not just literary types — whatever the trivial commercial message for Parrot's clothes cleaning. And that the ironic parting slogan expresses his disdain for the lies of advertising, and that is his real literary message. An accessible *coda* for his worldview. Possible, very possible!"

"Maybe it goes beyond that," Mary Louise said. "Mocking our human tendency to think we can perfectly fix all things on this sad old planet."

Luke had begun to pace, his full color back: "Good, very good. And in the same way, consider his riff on touched-up appearances versus painful reality: *'Trust your outsides to us. We'll cover for you — Solomon Parrot.'* The preceding jingle parts are plain fun. So he has his comedy, then follows with his tragic irony, expressing his own truth. Theodore Costas might have enjoyed himself here today after all!"

"And maybe not. We just can't know," Carol said. "But whatever any of us leave behind, the living will make sense of it as they like."

"True enough." Mary Louise looked into the face of this woman half a generation older than she and began to wish that she lived closer. "Back there, at the end of his little speech, Sol Jr proclaimed, 'What a legacy he has left!', and I thought it should be 'What legacy *has he* left?'

"Wait a minute," Luke said to Carol. "Didn't you say that what *he* liked to think of as his legacy was tutoring those kids after he retired?"

"That's right. And there he did admit his rhyming playfulness with words was the key to his success. He told me that many of them had come in hating words and reading."

"That would be plenty legacy for me," Mary Louise told them, thinking of the fog of lost memory at Heavenly Rest, in which she labored to contribute something memorable. "I hope and pray it's enough for him."

"Well, let's us three go drink a toast to that," Luke said. "I know an okay bar two blocks down."

Carol grinned at them. "Sounds good. He liked that kind of thing himself. Mr. Ted was a Christian believer in the after-life, and if he's right, I bet he'll be there looking down, toasting us too, cheering us on."

"Which we could surely use," Mary Louise said.

"Which we could surely use," her brother added.

So the three of them did that, and enjoyed an hour together in a dark corner of Sam's West End Brauhaus, drinking to Mr. Theodore Costas and all the yearnings for legacy.

Chapter Four:
Welcome Center

Just yesterday she had experienced such a heartening welcome in a distant town, and Carol thought maybe that was why she was especially stricken by this very different sight before her now on a Baltimore sidewalk. And maybe it was that recent generosity received which made her stop and not simply pass by.

In the late afternoon of yesterday she had spent an hour with a woman and her brother at a bar in a small city a hundred miles away, following the dedication of a memorial for Ted Costas. They had discussed the meaning of the old man's vanished life and what might be the meaning of their continuing ones. The brother she had met once briefly, when he had given her some boxes of Ted's things, and his sister she had met that day at the dedication, and yet … such closeness with them both, like fellow pilgrims in that small town bar. So much so that she hadn't been much surprised when — as they came out onto the sidewalk — the woman had invited her to dinner at home, and to stay over with her family so she wouldn't have to drive back to Baltimore by herself at night. And it had been good to stay with her.

But now to see this shockingly different sidewalk scene laid out before her! It seemed the reverse side of such human welcome — the ultimate picture of rejection, banishment.

At first she only pulled her car to the curb on the other side of the row house street and watched: an old-fashioned small pump organ, as might once have been played in a country church, had been deposited on the sidewalk, and before it sat a woman, bent forward — but obviously not to serenade the indifferent urban passersby. Instead, she was stretched out in an anguish of despair: arms thrown skyward and forehead pressed for support against the music rack. Her other belongings surrounded her on the pavement – a single bed, assorted small furniture, battered suitcase and trunk, bridge lamp with faded floral shade. Over it all, the woman's voice rose and died — keening as on a knife edge.

It was only eight in the morning — she might have been dragged from bed and dumped with all her earthly possessions onto this public sidewalk. Her body was pulled forward over the black and white keys as on a rack, and her taut back heaved with sobs.

Carol got out of her car and crossed the street.

"Blubbering again, Mildred? Phoning a mover would be a better use of your time!" This in a strident voice from a swaggering, broad-waisted woman in a shiny black dress who had just come out of the apartment door. This "Mildred" raised her head from the organ and cried mournfully, "Mover's not scheduled till Thursday. You said I could keep my things in the apartment till then!"

The other woman straightened and tilted her head high above the complaint: "Now you know I told you that was conditional on my new subtenant not needing it. Legally, it's been his apartment since Saturday. He's a man of business, his situation changed and he has to get moved in now — I told you that yesterday."

"But you only left the message. I would have told you it was too late — can't find any mover on Labor Day to come the next morning!"

The woman in the shiny black dress made no reply, but rummaged in her fat purse until she found a ring of keys.

"You have a new car, and money now!" the other pleaded. "Couldn't you just help me get my things moved before you go?"

"I'm a very busy woman. Today I have an appointment with the attorney about two lawsuits, and I'm having new furniture delivered to the condominium. I just stopped by here to let the man's movers in."

"Oh, Christ — you're acting *so mean*!"

This outburst from a young teenager in jeans, whom Carol had seen emerge from the little corner grocery opposite and had now come charging into the street.

The swaggering woman jerked around: "Joanie Rudgear, you watch your language and get back in the car if you want me to take you to school!"

A big man in a sleeveless tee shirt came out of the apartment building and plopped down on the sidewalk an old-style hat rack. "That's the last of your things, M'am," he told the woman slumped at the organ.

"How much I owe you?"

He looked embarrassed. "I guess sixty dollars would be enough. I'd do it for less, but I got to give my partner thirty for helping me down with the organ and the bed."

This "Joanie", likely the daughter of the swaggering woman, had now reached the sidewalk and stood in her worn jeans, patched at the knees, and an army fatigue shirt flapping loose at her hips — left hand pointing at the accumulated furniture and right hand on an ice cream cone — and laid into her mother: "Look at this, all over the pavement! It's like Miss Mildred's whole life spread out in front of everyone, 'cause she told me these things go way back in her family and like that — and you couldn't care less how she feels!"

"Last chance, Missy, if you want a ride to school from me."

"I'd rather walk it on my own!"

The woman shrugged. "Okay, but you better start now. It'll take you fifteen minutes at least, and I'm not writing you no lateness note."

Carol watched as the woman strode across the street and got into a big new Cadillac SUV, which looked almost as broad-beamed, shiny, swaggering and tasteless as she did.

This Mildred handed a rumpled check to the mover. "It'll be good by Friday. Please wait till then to cash it."

Ignoring her disappearing mother, Joanie began stroking Mildred's arm as she sat slumped at the organ: "Sorrryy."

Carol had to step aside quickly for the two movers headed toward the apartment building with a leatherette couch for the incoming businessman.

"Who are *you*?"

The teenager had turned from Mildred to confront her.

"One who would like to help." In the pause that followed, they both studied her face. "I was just driving through, but this is quite a scene. I had to stop and offer something."

"Like what?" this teenager challenged.

"I'm so embarrassed to be here like this in front of everyone with my things thrown out and no way to move them!" Mildred burst out. "But I was told I could stay till Thursday."

"I know. I understand that." Then Carol turned to the girl. "What I can offer is to come back here with a pick-up truck and move this furniture into safe storage."

"Storage where?" Mildred looked a little suspicious now.

"At my house."

At that all four eyes stared at her. "It's easy for me," Carol added. "I have a small time furniture restoration business, so we have a secure storage building in back — and a truck to move customers' stuff. It won't be difficult."

"For how much, and how can she know to trust you?" Joanie asked, but not hostilely — more like a carefulness learned from her mother.

Carol went into her purse, found a business card and gave it to Mildred. "That's my home as well as business address. It's right in the neighborhood, less than a mile from here, Garret street near Brownlow Avenue. No charge."

Mildred lowered her eyes. "I do trust you, hon. Thank you so for helping a woman in need." She dabbed at her cheeks and stood up from the organ, a little shaky.

"Good. I have to go to my husband's work in Hampden and change cars with him. Then I'll come back here with the truck — take maybe forty minutes, I'm guessing."

"Miss Mildred, you want I should wait with you till she comes back?"

"Naw, honey. I be all right. You go on to school, like your mom said."

"Okay, but I don't anymore care what she says. That woman is a government certified..." She shook her head, as though it was beyond her to say what, but she slung on her backpack and headed off down the sidewalk.

On the way to Larry's office to exchange vehicles, Carol called on her cell to let him know. He was happy to get his car back in preference to the junky old truck she used in her refinishing business but had not wanted to drive the three hundred miles round trip to the Ted Costas memorial.

Her estimate had been good: in just forty-one minutes she was back at the sad scene where Mildred sat among her things dumped on the sidewalk.

Luckily, the movers were still there, carrying the new tenant's furniture into the building, and readily agreed to lift Mildred's two heavy pieces, the organ and an old-fashioned bed, onto the truck. She and Mildred did the rest, and then Carol opened the passenger door and helped her up the step and in.

"Why don't we go straight to my house?" she suggested. "That way you can see where your furniture is going to live for a while — in safe storage. Then I'll drop you and your luggage wherever you're staying."

"You're mighty kind." Mildred drew a deep breath and glanced around, as though resetting some internal control. "I'm feeling real different now, thanks to you. Thinking this might be the best thing for me. That woman was hard to live with. She'll chew you out for nothing. Hard for her daughter too, with a mom like that and her dad passed on. I try to help her feel good in herself, but she has to keep fighting off that woman."

"I can see that."

"I plan to stay at the YW until I find a place. Have a reservation for Thursday, but they might could fit me in today." Mildred paused, a mousy- looking little woman but seeming quite revived in spirit.

"If my stuff is crowding you too much, you let me know, and I'll get it moved to one of those storage locker places. That's where I was planning to put it, but saving the money comes in pretty good now. But it's more than money. I think living with her was starting to do me in — why I got so wasted when she put me on the street this morning. You got me breathing good air again, hon!"

"I can see that, and I'm very glad."

"True, everybody has got things in their life causes them to be the way they are, but with that Robyn Rudgear it's hard to know what could have made her so. You know her little daughter you saw is still mourning her great uncle who died at age ninety some months ago, but her mother didn't care one thing about him. Except getting him out of the apartment he loved from the years there with his wife, and sticking him in a cheap nursing home so she wouldn't have to bother with him. He outfoxed her though. The morning she was coming to get him from the hospital and plop him in that place, he bolted early and took a train all the way to Florida to escape his fate. Died the same day he arrived there, poor soul. But she didn't care about that either. Only thing mattered to her was that now she could sue for big bucks — the Baltimore Orioles because he died at their Florida stadium and the Hopkins Hospital because he escaped from there. And inheriting his money through Joanie — *that* mattered to her. Though I believe she'll get a lot more from the lawsuits. She fixing to be a rich woman."

Carol pulled into her driveway and turned off the engine but made no movement to get out. Instead, she turned slowly toward her passenger.

"Now I know what woman we're talking about. She wanted to run Ted Costas' life, really to end it for him."

Mildred was staring at her.

"I don't know how much you ever talked to him…"

"I did some. A good man. Once in a while Robyn would bring him to the apartment when they were doing some errand, and we two would be left together a few minutes, while she made a phone call or the like."

"His best buddy left in the world was my dad," Carol told her. "The two of them would eat together regularly at Thatcher's Bar and Grill on Ludlow Avenue. I loved that old man."

Mildred waited a respectful moment and then commented, "It's a peculiar small world in this neighborhood. You and your husband are living here and connected to Mr. Costas through your dad, but Robyn, Joanie and I don't know about you and you don't know about us."

"We're all connected through Ted Costas," Carol said. "He's the one who is no longer on this earth, but he's at the center of much still going on."

A sharp rapping on Mildred's window, and the woman started back: a face pressed flat against the glass, mouth and nose making an ugly monster.

"Don't worry – that's just Sam, my mover come to unload your things. One of his cute tricks." He had brought Ben with him, as Carol had suggested this was a two-man job. She unlocked the shed for them, and they moved in the organ, the bed, and a chest of drawers, while she and Mildred brought the lighter things.

"Come in, and I'll fix us some breakfast," Carol told her. She felt a strong urge to be welcoming to this woman, to neutralize that stark earlier scene of inhospitality on the public street.

"Thank you so much. Let me call the YW first, to tell them I want a room for the two extra nights until Thursday, before they all get taken."

The thought came to Carol, and she hesitated only a moment: "Oh, why don't you stay with us those two nights? We have an extra bedroom now my daughter is off to college."

Mildred ducked her head. "You've done so much already. That's so sweet, but…"

"My husband Larry liked Ted Costas too, and it would give us both a chance to hear what you knew of him — since you shared that apartment with his nephew's widow."

"Well, I didn't hear much about him from her, except complaints, until the day he escaped from the hospital and ran away to Florida. But then she got all interested, because she was fixing to sue for a pot of money. But Joanie, his only remaining kin — she cared about him and told me things."

"Good. So you will stay with us, until your reservation at the YW?"

"Thank you, being so kind. You saw me back there on that pavement. You know this is one day in my life I can use some of that."

Carol fixed breakfast for them and told her about yesterday and the memorial dedication to Mr. Ted as the "Jinglist and Poet". Then she took her upstairs to the spare bedroom, and left her to unpack and take a nap from the tension of the morning. She set an alarm to wake her shortly before noon, so she could walk to her nearby job at the St. Vincent Thrift Shop.

After a couple of hours work out in the shed on furniture, Carol realized that she could use a nap herself. It had been an early morning departure from the house of Mary Louise Botts a hundred and fifty miles away, where she herself had been the one so welcomed and put up for the night.

From a deep sleep she was awakened by the sound of knocking on the street door. It wouldn't be Mildred, because she had been given a key and would still be working at the Thrift Store, and their sign against solicitations usually repelled door-to door salesmen. Carol gave a quick brush to her hair and went down, a little curious.

She peered out the glass side panel and saw two slender legs in worn blue jeans with heart patches on the knees. The person's head was turned away, so she couldn't see the face, but now she had a premonition.

"Hi, Joanie," she said, opening the door.

The girl looked surprised. "Oh, you remembered my name."

"Of course. And you remembered my address from my business card. Good for you. Please come in."

This morning, so upset with the sidewalk scene, she had seemed more grown-up, but now she was all the embarrassed, uncertain early teenager – with a small doll, it seemed, tied into her pony tail like a good luck charm.

"Just wanted to make sure Miss Mildred and her stuff got here okay."

"Yes, she's off at work now, but would you like to see our furniture shed, where her things are in temporary residence?"

Yes, she would. Carol had thought it would give her something to do and relieve her awkwardness.

Once she had seen Mildred's furniture safely stored, Joanie looked around at the other pieces in process. "So you fix up all these yourself?"

"Yep. I do the carpentry when the wooden structure needs reinforcing. But more often I just re-finish the surfaces."

"So why is doing that to the surfaces a thing people want?"

"Oh, have you ever seen where folks leave drinks that make rings on a table? Sometimes I just re-do the surface to take that off. Other times, people decide they want to show everyone a whole different wood tone on their dining room table, say — who knows why? I guess the same reason people want to change their own surfaces — want a new sun tan or a new dress to impress everyone with how cool they are."

Joanie grinned, pleased with that. "Yeah, yeah. That's psychology, and I'm interested in that.

Actually today I was reading up on it."

"You're studying it in class?"

Joanie glanced off at the high window of the shed, and didn't reply.

Then suddenly she blurted: "Miss Mildred — did she find a place to stay until her Thursday reservation at the YW?"

"I asked her to stay here with us until then, and she agreed."

"Wow. And you don't even know her! And meantime, my mother, who does — she tells the movers this morning, 'Go ahead and put her on the sidewalk. She has no legal rights in this unit.'" Joanie whipped her head back and forth, trying to deal with it. "This morning you're stopping by to help like a good Samaritan — and meantime, she's acting like a government certified … Darth Vader!"

Remembering the woman's outfit on the sidewalk this morning, Carol had to smile: she and the movie villain both did go in for your basic black. "You know," Joanie pursued, "since she's coming into all this money from the lawsuits, it's just making her worse. Exactly what it's doing!"

"Maybe the loss of your great uncle has upset her more than she shows."

"No way — she didn't care for him at all. But who does she care for!"

"Well, you may not know that my father, who was Thomas Curry and died in January, was an old buddy of your uncle. They used to eat out together at Thatcher's, on Ludlow."

"That was *your* dad? I used to hear of him."

"Through my dad I knew your Uncle Ted. I loved knowing him."

Joanie shook her head wonderingly. "I really miss him."

The look in her face caused Carol to remember: "Look, I have some of his things you could look through! Haven't had time to do that myself. When your mom ... That is, when his apartment was cleared out, a man whose family business had valued him as an advertising consultant got the furniture jobber to let him take some stuff that was left behind in Mr. Ted's drawers and trunks. He came here hoping to talk to my dad. Of course too late for that, but when I told him that I had cared for Mr. Ted too, he gave me the boxes of his stuff."

Joanie was up for this right away, and Carol led her down to the basement room where she had it all stored.

"I have to go upstairs and work on some records for the business, but it's all in those boxes. Help yourself."

But Joanie was already kneeling eagerly on the floor, going at the first box.

Carol worked until she heard a key in the front door, and then went to greet Mildred returned from her job. She fixed tea for her, and they had both settled down in the cozy corner of the living room when they heard an on-rushing rumble pounding up the basement stairs toward them.

"Look at this photo!" Joanie called, bursting into the room.

Carol recognized it instantly. "That was my dad's eightieth birthday party, about ten years ago."

"And that's Uncle Ted and Aunt Tilda," Joanie said. "But what's with the alligator suits?"

Carol grinned. "I had both couples over here for that party. Your Uncle had just had *his* eightieth about two months earlier. The two old guys had this club they had made up — 'the Swamp Dwellers Society'. I don't know why — what it was about — but they were always kidding each other which one was the alligator and which one was the crocodile."

"What's the difference," Mildred said. "Why should they care?"

"Well, they always said the alligator just 'feasted on small mammals' but the crocodile 'ate human flesh'. Each claimed the other was the crocodile, and it was all in fun, but that's all I know about it."

That made everyone want to ogle the photo more closely. It really was a funny picture, Carol thought. Larry had taken it, and both old men looked so pleased with themselves to be in these alligator suits, with only their faces showing and their long-toothed snouts hanging down over their foreheads. "Wow — where did they get those realistic animal suits?" Joanie was clearly impressed.

"I got them," Carol said. "Knowing their old joke about that, I went to a theatrical supply store downtown and rented them. They loved it."

"Now I think I slightly remember Uncle Ted telling about that."

"This is a pretty nostalgic photo," Carol said more soberly. "Because both wives were still in good health then. My mom died only a year later, but your Uncle Ted's Estelle — for her it was only about two years ago?"

Joanie nodded. "Correct. But it's so cool you did this for them."

"Glad you dug it out. Really brings it back."

"I've got to go home soon, before Darthie gets there, but I want to look a few more minutes downstairs."

"Who's Dorothy?" Mildred asked.

"Sounds like 'Dorothy'," Joanie said, "but it's not that. You know Darth Vader from the movies? Mom's the female version, 'Darthie Vader'." Joanie went back downstairs to sift through her uncle's leavings, and shortly after Larry came home from work. Carol had warned him that they would have a house guest the next couple of days, which was fine with him — especially when he heard that she knew something of that eventful last day on earth of Ted Costas. He got a beer from the kitchen and sat to hear of the cruel sidewalk scene carried out less than a mile from here this very morning.

Again the sound of footsteps ascending from the basement. Only this time not charging up with teenage excitement but moving slow and stately.

Once she entered the room, Carol thought Joanie's face looked awed and beautiful.

"See what I found." Her voice was hushed, reverent. "It was in this envelope with my name on it."

She first extended them the paper. Carol took it, easily deciphered the hand-written script and read aloud: "This I gave to my beloved wife, Estelle in 1941. Since her death, I've kept it to feel her close, but it's saved for my great niece, Joan Rudgear. Dear

Joan, this ring is for your future life. Much love forever. Uncle Ted."

In the tears and excitement they all lost track of time, until a cell phone squawked and the present intruded.

Joanie put it to her ear and turned way.

"Yes...yes... very soon." She hung up.

"The mom. She's really mad I'm not home on time."

She ran downstairs to get her backpack, but returned not to the living room, where they all were, but to the shadows of the hall, making secret signals as though playing a spy in some mystery movie.

When Carol came to her, leaving Mildred and Larry talking, Joanie even stepped backward into the dining room so that the two of them were out of sight of the other two.

"Miss Carol, I want to ask a big favor of you. To drive me home, because the school bus has gone, and I don't know how to get there since we just moved two days ago."

"Where is it?"

"It's on the water in Canton. I've got the address."

"Yes, I could do that. You missed the school bus because you decided to come here to check on Mildred?"

She looked down for a second, then abruptly straight at her. "I did want to check Mildred, but I came to see you."

Carol asked her to wait and told the others where she was going. Once they were in the car, the girl resumed. "After this morning, I wanted to know you. That's why I came here, and I'm glad I did — and not just for the ring from Uncle Ted! Though that's so great. You know, I feel like a different person from that — like I've got a future now."

"I'm glad. Of course, you always had a future, but I know what you mean."

"What you do in that shop, all on your own – that's so neat and you dress cool like an artist, but not like you're trying to look young. If I could, I want to come back and see you sometimes. Would that be okay?"

"Sure. I might even put you to work in the shop a little."

"Would you? That would be so awesome!" But now she was hesitating. Something else she was working up to, Carol could see.

"But we might have to do something so that could happen."

"What's that, Joanie?"

"Oh, would you mind just calling me 'Joan'? It's my mom started that "Joanie" stuff. Uncle Ted always called me Joan."

"Okay, Joan. Go ahead."

"When we get to the new apartment, if you could sort of march me in there and tell Darthie that you caught me hooking school and thought you should bring me home. That would do it. And you wouldn't be lying — I did hook school today."

"But how would I have known you? I never saw you until today."

"You did know me through Uncle Ted, a friend of yours — right?"

"Well, I knew *of* you. He did talk about you. So I guess I could say as a friend of Ted's, I knew he wouldn't approve of your cutting school."

"Right! There you go — that'll work great!"

"One thing, Joan. I'm not going to lie about this. Any straight question she asks me, I'm going to tell her the truth."

"Okay, if she does. But she usually doesn't care enough to ask the details, unless something makes her suspicious."

Once she agreed to the plan, the girl seemed very happy. "See, if she thinks you're one who's going to kick my butt when I do wrong, then she's going to have no problem with me seeing you. For Darthie, if you're tough on me, then you must be a good influence."

"What have I got myself into here?" said Carol, only half-laughing.

"Oh nothing — don't worry. I won't crowd you. I know everyone needs space."

The condominium apartment building was quite plush and looked almost new. She and Joanie rode in the elevator to one of the top floors. Carol made some comment about how luxurious it seemed. "Yeah, it's fancy, but I tell you she's worse here than she was on Crossley Street."

When they got to apartment 20 C, there was a note taped to the door.

I can be found on the penthouse deck.
Robyn Rudgear

"Should we go there?" Carol asked.

Joanie was shaking her head. "No, she doesn't mean me to go there. She means some of her new rich neighbors — who she doesn't know any but hopes they'll want to meet her. So far seems like there's no line forming."

She had taken off her backpack, unzipped a small pocket and taken out the door key. "I'll go dig in like crazy on my homework. Meantime, you go there — that's it! You're there to report me, and she'll be glad to see you, being like an actual person is coming to that fancy place to look her up. That's perfect. You remember what she looks like from this morning?"

"Oh, yes." Carol hesitated. "I will do this for you, Joan. And I would like to see you again too. But I hope you can get on a better footing with your mother. Even grownups who can seem so cocky are afraid of things, and that can make them act…not the best."

"Right. I know that's psychology, interesting stuff I'm going to read up on more." Carol had waved and started to move off, but Joanie called after her, "I wasn't lying to you before — I *was* reading up on psychology today like I said. Only it was in the public library, not the school."

Following her directions, Carol took the elevator up one more floor, to the penthouse. She would do this for Joan, but also for herself. There was something she could contribute here, as long as she could keep the mother from seeing her as the enemy.

The elevator opened into an imitation of a lush tropical garden. Couples and foursomes sat with drinks at glass umbrella tables with potted palms, fake Poinciana and imitation orchids, all arranged around a little fountain being continually regurgitated from the mouth of a hideous brass frog. At the far end sat a Jacuzzi and a wading pool, though no one was there. A large sign on the wall in lacquered bamboo proclaimed "Welcome Center".

Carol spotted Ms. Robyn Rudgear in a minute. She sat alone at one of the glass tables, sipping a drink. She was not reading anything but staring out. Her chair too was turned out, and the one beside it, as though to welcome company, but there were no takers. As Joanie had said, "so far, no line forming."

And her face did not invite anyone. Though she had arranged the chairs and herself to suggest openness to company, she apparently could not alter the expression on her face — or was unaware of it. The lips seemed compressed as though holding in anger, and the eyes were narrowed with ready suspicion.

This fancy place was her prize for the lawsuit settlements, the smaller inheritance coming from Ted Costas, and her general machinations in her own interest, but now she sat alone and miserable looking beneath that "Welcome Center" in gold-stained bamboo. She welcomed no one, and no one welcomed her.

In a another moment Carol would go to her and "report on" Joanie's truancy from school that day, introducing herself as someone who slightly knew the girl from Ted Costas — and being careful not to sound too affectionate toward him either — and who thought from what she had heard of her mother, that she would want to know about the skipping school. She would do that in minute, but not yet. For a moment longer she would stand here, taking in this painful scene. This poor woman, so un- welcomed in this shiny Welcome Center. So human and so lost. It was a picture, as they say, worth a thousand words.

Chapter Five:
What Father Now?

Security people were always warning you about a stranger sneaking something into your luggage, Seth thought, but not like this. No damaging boom of fire and shrapnel had followed his touching this inserted item, but looking back he would have to say it had sure let loose an explosion of intriguing mystery that had filled the days of his spring vacation.

And he could use that, it turned out, because on that first morning home in Savannah his girlfriend Lindsey called him early enough that he thought something must be wrong.

"Hey boy, I don't have the best of news." She had gone on to explain how some aunt in the family was serious sick in Valdosta, and they were all going down there to help out.

"Oh, sorry. When do you get back?"

"Likely not till late Thursday night."

"Ungood. Very ungood."

"Right, but we'll at least have Friday and Saturday before we go back to school."

That was looking on the bright side, which Seth found hard to do. Since his Dad had died fifteen months ago, his time at home was less fun and even a little strained, as his mom worked five and a half days a week and then tried hard to entertain him when she was home. She didn't really have the energy left over for that, and he tried to tell her to relax, but it seemed like both of them sensed too much that something was missing. Namely his father.

And his best friends from high school wouldn't be around, as their Spring Break had been the week before.

Today his mom worked only until noon, and then she wanted to take him out to lunch at an Old Savannah restaurant they both liked. Dinner was expensive for her budget now that his dad was gone, so they would go for lunch.

After he had shaved and showered to be ready for that, he decided to finish unpacking his shoulder bag, and that was when he discovered the gentle explosive device, a time bomb that would keep firing over the next several days – and likely much longer. In the zipped side pocket he had put a few things to have handy on the train. He removed the train schedule, paperback novel, pens and small notebook, but then he saw a colored envelope pressed against the inside wall of the bag. What was that?

He took it out and saw that it was an Amtrak ticket envelope with his first name hand-printed on the front. Not his own printing.

Nothing inside – empty. But now, flipping it over, he saw on the blank backside a message, small-printed in the same quick hand lettering:

True sympathy on your father's recent death.
Lost mine when I was young as well. 1930s —
courted a girl in Savannah, 1100 Edmund. Back
yard under big trees — family burial ground and big
bell-shaped stone. Upon it wonderful poem carved,
on finding father when your natural one taken.
Title — "What Father Now?" Helped me some —
pray it may help you.

Seth had no doubt that it was the old man on the train who had slipped the envelope into this outside pocket of his shoulder bag. An interesting character, he had been seated at the table in the dining car with Lindsey and him and had paid for their dinner in exchange for their answering questions for a survey of college students he said he was doing.

A mixed reaction to this hidden note. Now a grown man of twenty-one, he had become quite tired of older people offering him wise advice and suggestions. On the other hand, this old man had been unusually appealing: he had told them he was ninety, so he had seventy years experience on them, and yet he had treated Lindsey and him as equals in rare style — he sort of tip-toed up to you.

He put the note away and resumed dressing for lunch with his mother.

At the restaurant they sat outside in a rear garden, and Seth was reminded of the old man's note — the house with the family burial plot in back, under old shade trees like these. He and his mother had a pretty good time, though with them there was always now an underlying emptiness.

After they had ordered dessert, Seth asked her where Edmund street or road or avenue was in Savannah. She had lived here all her life and knew most everything about it.

But she was shaking her head. "I can't recall ever hearing of that."

"You sure?"

"Unless it's a tiny little glorified alley somewhere, I don't think it exists in this city."

Maybe that had made it a challenge. When he got home, he got out the street atlas to check her. No — no Edmund anything. Surprisingly frustrating. To go check that out would have given him a little adventure to kill some time until he could make himself study or Lindsey got back, whichever came first.

Instead, he went onto the Internet to check a couple of history websites which he had been trolling for term paper ideas. He had two courses where his initial proposal would be due soon after his return.

In the midst of that, it struck him — "Come on, Mr. History Major, you know street names do get changed and disappear!" With some excitement he did an Internet search for "Edmund" as a street in Savannah to see if there was any historical reference to it.

Nothing.

Seth retrieved the old man's note from his shoulder bag. At age ninety, he might easily have misremembered the name. Anyway, it had led to a dead end – might as well toss it. He held it above the wastebasket, hesitated, and noticed some scribbling on the other side. Hard to read – he turned on his desk lamp to study it.

One line was clear: "North Carolina State" – he and Lindsey's university. Then, "Weekend travel, when they can afford." And here it said, "Conflict – she wants things done faster." Ah–these were the notes he had taken from interviewing them in the dining car. For the survey he said he was doing of college students.

Seth thoughtfully dropped the envelope into his desk drawer. It had seemed odd to him at the time that the old man had no prepared form or even blank paper to take these notes on. And now, even more...

It was certainly possible that a ninety year old man had misplaced his regular paper to take the survey on, Seth thought, and used the Amtrak envelope as an expedient, and then forgotten that these notes were on the back when jotting a message on the front and slipping it into his shoulder bag, but...

But Seth was struck by another possibility: maybe the whole survey was a fake. Then these rough notes would only have been to make it look real, and that was why he hadn't been more careful with them. And the old man had seemed to remember from his own college days the money problems of students. It had seemed like he saw himself in them. Then maybe he just really wanted to buy them dinner. He had made up that survey business so he could do it without embarrassing them.

The more he thought about it, the more that seemed likely. He had clearly shown this kind intent toward them. And then, when he had learned that Seth, like him, had lost his father at a young age, he had wanted to give him something more – the tombstone poem. When had he slipped it into that outside pocket of his bag?

He should pursue this further. Probably what he should do is go down to City Hall when it opened on

Monday and find out if there ever was an Edmund, and if so where. In seventy years the name could have been changed, or if a little street it could have been closed and the land built over. But the big tombstone with the father poem might still be there.

Wait a minute — seventy years to remember the exact name! What if the old man had slightly misremembered it? He quickly returned to the atlas.

There was no "Edmund" but there was an "Edlund"! Ah, that would make sense, just one letter different, and "Edmund" was so much more common that anyone's brain could easily make that switch — much less a ninety year old's!

What a Sherlock Holmes I'm becoming!

He asked his mother to borrow the car, and she agreed but with a tentative voice that told him she wanted to know why. Good she didn't actually ask because there was something here related to the loss of his dad that he would rather keep private.

According to the map, Edlund wasn't in the oldest part of the city but adjacent to the Victorian area built some decades later. Actually fringe to that. Once on the scene, he found that Edlund Street was only two blocks long and falling into decay — some shabby houses and several vacant lots on which the buildings had likely been torn down. There were only two readable street numbers, and they were in the

300's, so how could it have contained "1100"? But on such a small street, numbering might have been different seventy years ago.

There was one house it might possibly be. It was paint-less and boarded up but might have been attractive once. And it did have a spacious rear yard, protected by a crumbling stucco wall and overhung by large Water Oaks. He parked the car, to give it a try.

As he stepped over wall rubble into what would have been the rear garden, Seth paused. He was trying to imagine the old man at his own age, sharing a supper here with the girl he had been "courting" and her family. Way back in the decade of the "Great Depression". The old man had recalled a little of that era for Lindsey and him last night on the train. But what was this eerie, touched feeling that came over him now when he thought of the man here at his own age, seventy years before? Sadness, tenderness — imagining a time when he himself would be that old and an abandoned place like this would be all that was left of some such sweet memory?

This former garden was littered with mess: beer cans, trash and broken children's toys. There were many of these, suggesting the house might last have served as a little school, and this had been the playground.

And there, near the corner of the garden was a curved gray shape. Seth stared, moved closer — and still it seemed that the flat gray shape lying flush on the ground could really be a fallen tombstone, curved at the top like a bell!

His heart was racing as he knelt beside it. Vines overgrew it, plant litter covered it. Would he be able to pry the heavy stone out of the ground to read the inscription on the other side?

His fingers closed tight on the edge, ready to tug hard.

But now it bent inward under the pressure of his fingers. It was not a stone, but a piece of gray plastic, which — once he broke the suction with the earth — popped up in his face. He stood it on end and saw on its earth side — showing through the dirt clumps, worms and dead grass — a familiar, faded caricature.

All too clear now, this icon of the cartoon world: Bugs Bunny munching on standard carrot. No profound poetry on finding a father replacement, but the comic rabbit posing in conversation balloon his own eternal question: "What's up, Doc?"

On the drive back home, stopped at a traffic light, Seth sang out: "*So what is up?*" Seemed he was running every which way, looking for something. And he had been so ready to believe that a stranger's note hidden in his suitcase might provide that. And even now, to admit the truth, he still clung to that image of a poem-engraved headstone with a profound message just for him.

That feeling was strong enough that he didn't even miss Lindsay as much, though he still counted himself super lucky because she was the absolute cutest girl he'd ever seen and he just an average looking guy, though she did like that he was big and had lots of curly brown hair.

Sunday he celebrated his mother's birthday. He bought a small version of her favorite cake — Orange — and gave her a picture book he had bought with money saved from last summer's job. It was *Nineteenth Century American Quilting,* with lots of gorgeous color photos which he had known would blow her away. She had done some of that herself, and had a long time interest in women's home crafts of earlier times. But when night came, he grew restless and knew for sure that he wasn't done with the headstone.

Monday morning he dropped his mother at her job and was at the Public Works Department in City Hall before ten. He explained only that he was looking for an old house with some interesting history, to see if it was still standing. The clerk began shaking his head as soon as he said "1100 Edmund street, road, avenue — whatever."

"I've worked here forty years, and that's never been a street name in Savannah."

"I believe you, but I'm thinking further back. My reference to that address is from the 1930s."

"I'm pretty sure not. But we have old property books, and I can look there. Come along — you can check it yourself."

Seth followed him into a large rear room. The man pulled a big bound portfolio book off a high shelf and set it on a table. He began turning over the pages, alphabetical by street address. In a moment it became clear that there had been no Edmund anything.

"How about Edward and Edlund?" Seth asked him.

There was no Edward, and the numbers on Edlund were 300s and 400s only – just the two disappointing blocks he had investigated Saturday.

"Could the numbers on Edlund have changed, so that there might actually have been an 1100 in the 1930s?"

"Not possible. All streets have been numbered in the grid system, based on blocks from the zero coordinate streets. Once assigned, they don't change."

Seth thought his face must have shown his unhappiness, based on how the clerk's expression now shifted. "Look, Bud. If this is real important to you, don't give up with just Savannah."

"What do you mean? My source said the house was here."

The clerk shrugged. "Well, in these offices we're exact about the city limits, but the average person isn't. Someone may say 'Savannah' but just mean the general area. If I was you, I'd check Chatham County."

"That makes a lot of sense. Thanks so much."

And he was even more excited when at the county offices he found that there *was* an Edmund Street, in the old village of Laurel Dell, just a few miles outside the city limits. Again the street numbers were too low to include 1100, but the clerk told him that there had been no systematic numbering years ago, and that the addresses had changed on many of the older roads.

By noon, Seth was cruising down the four blocks of Edmund Street in Laurel Dell, checking possibilities. Most of the houses were little post World War II brick ranchers, but in the same block there was a large old stone house that was plenty old enough to have been there in the thirties, and a smaller two story frame one that might be old enough. Both did have tree-shaded, rear gardens that looked like they could be hiding an overgrown family burial plot.

He parked and walked up the front steps and onto the covered porch of the larger house. An historical plaque near the front door said it had been built "Circa 1840". Way old enough.

He knocked, and a voice cried harshly: "Enter the scene!"

Inside, Seth confronted a fifty-something man with long side-whiskers seated oddly at a small desk in the front hall and staring sharply at him. He suddenly winked and said, "Certified Enacter, or I missed my guess!"

"Well, I'm interested in the history of the house."

"Dressing?"

"Sir?"

"Pardon the presumption. Now I see you tote no duds. So, spectator and witness to our world — that's what you would be."

Seth nodded vaguely. "Yes, but I'll just check out the back garden if you don't mind."

The man's gray side-whiskers worked up and down beside the grimacing eyes. "Can't wait for the re-enactment, eh? No – too hot about the signs of dastardly invaders back there. Still filled with righteous fury, you are!"

Seth hesitated, but before he could ask what the man meant, he stood abruptly at the desk and clacked together his boots: "Sgt. Herman Funk, Irregular of the Georgia Resistance!" Decisively, he put out his hand to be shaken, and Seth complied.

"Young man, your interest does you credit. To you the glorious past is no mere earthen vessel in a state of worm-eaten decay — I can see that. Duds-less you may be now, but I see ahead in the not distant future the day you join us. As a cannoneer, right? That's your ticket!"

"I've heard that can cause deafness," Seth said insanely, as though ready to enlist.

"Say a cavalryman then. Prefer the jarring gallop over rock-ribbed earth in preference to horrific explosions in the ear. That's you!"

A rustle on the stairs and Seth looked up to see a vision out of a romance novel. A pretty woman was descending in an old-fashioned flowing dress, hair done up in tassels.

And now a side door opened and an obese older man in the uniform of a Confederate general came out, brandishing his saber. "Where are the others? Late, are they? Better take care, or I'll slice them to size!"

"Somewhat, General. Now you're here, you take over the desk, and I'll go and dress. Fill this young man in on the history of this here site. He's not one to wait patient for the enactment — not him!"

"Lt. Lemuel 'Beeswax' Shultz, Sherman's man, commandeered this house as his headquarters. Chased out the Confederate widow and her children!" the man fumed over his big belly. "Like she had no rights at all." Seth felt better when the man slid his sword into the scabbard hanging from his belt. "But the common folk of the Dell here gave him a taste of his own strong medicine. Cut off his food supply. The last month in this house, he lived on moldy rice. Till one morning he hobbled out with his remaining soldiers that hadn't sneaked off, and begged for our mercy. We gave it to him — and a rasher of bacon — and put him on the one train that still could run out of Savannah 'cause the Yankee soldiers hadn't gotten around to blowing up its locomotive yet."

"That was the last time a Union soldier set foot in this house," another man, who had just entered in full uniform, finished for him.

To Seth it was now clear that getting any history about this house not focused on 1861-65 would be, for the moment, quite challenging.

He thought about going into the garden for the coming re-enactment of the occupation by the Union commander of the house and his eventual banishment with bacon — at least he could surreptitiously look for a bell-shaped tombstone — but then he saw a better opportunity. The pretty woman who had come downstairs in full ball gown seemed well disposed to him, and here was a chance to get her aside.

"What about the 1930s?" he asked her. "Where can I find out about the family that lived here then?"

"Honey, nobody has lived here but a caretaker since the 1890s. Since then it's been a museum house on the war, run by the Daughters of the Confederacy."

Cross this one off.

"You come back and see us, though," the woman was saying. "Everyone gets a role to play and a chance to shine."

Seth knew this was not his drama or cast of fellow players, but he was surely looking for his role to play in history — modern version — versus just reading about it all the time.

He walked a block to check out the other two-story house. From the looks of it, it might be just old enough to have been here in the 1930s.

Approaching the steps, he noticed a curious sign beside the front door: "The Glorious Lightning" in gold lettering, surrounded by wavy rays.

He rang the bell and waited some time before he heard slow steps approaching.

Suddenly the door swung open, and there was quite an old lady wearing quite a wide smile. "Enter, young man, enter! We're delighted you have come to us."

He stepped into what would have been the living room of any normal house. Now he sensed two other old ladies moving toward him, but he had no visual field left over for them.

The room itself, and its adjacent hall, had taken him over.

Walls and ceiling were painted or papered in the brightest iridescent colors — mostly tones of gold, but also intense reds and oranges against a background of sky blue. And set about on low tables were queer, old-looking electrical machines which, behind glass, circulated rippling waves of liquid light — oily, undulating stripes in fantastic, bright-hued motion.

"Good Lord!" he exclaimed.

"None of that," pronounced the old lady who had admitted him.

"Yes, truly it is the Scientific Being of Electricity."

"The Stream of Eternal Radiational Energy," the third old lady put in, "into which anyone may dip a hand."

The three women — the word "crones" occurred to him, but that would have been not just unkind but unfair: these ladies were not at all grim or witchlike. Their faces shone on him as though in imitation of the electrical light of the wave motion machines — fluttery like that, and determinedly bright.

"What *is* this?"

"*The Glorious Lightning*"! Their voices were nearly in unison.

"Of course, we have the whole grand story here," one lady said. "A vast amount of literature for your perusal, any time you may wish to come."

"And of course tracts and pamphlets for you to study at home."

"But what's this 'Glorious Lightning'", Seth asked them.

"That was how he described it," the door-opening lady replied.

"Who?"

"Billy Bunton. He was an ordinary out-of-work pipe fitter in the small, Great Smokies town of Terminal, Tennessee in 1937. The height of the Depression, you know."

"And he had his own depression." The third old lady had picked up the story, reciting with enthusiasm, but as though for the thousandth time. "Out of work, with a wife and two children to support." The three of them had closed about Seth where he stood, all very much shorter, ringing him with eager upturned faces.

"But then it happened."

"What was that?"

"He was struck by lightning."

"Not in Terminal," the first old lady explained. "But on the mountain top where he had gone to meditate about the fate of himself and his family."

"It changed from a Great Smoky Mountain then into an absolutely clear mountain. It was nighttime, but the bolt of lightning flashing down 'made everything as clear as day'. This was how Billy always explained it while he yet lived."

There was now some pounding, rumbling sound, Seth thought, which seemed to threaten the house.

Suddenly, the old ladies heard it, and screamed. The door opener ran to the side window and threw up the shade. "Julia, they're in your dahlias again, the brutes!"

"What's that!" Seth cried over the noise from without and the lady screams from within.

"Those blundering Confederates!" This from the one who had been the quietest of the three until now, but suddenly rushed to another window, threw it up and began to gesture violently outside at the passing horsemen with a long, black pointed umbrella. "Keep to the stream, you Vermin!" she shouted. "Off this property!"

Even the pretty woman in the ball gown was on horseback now, Seth could see — riding side saddle at a trot — behind the men who were cantering along, brandishing a battle flag, down by the trees at the bottom of the slope.

"What are they doing?" he asked.

"Oh, they're re-enacting, re-enacting, forever re-enacting! The rail line ran beside the stream there, and they're putting the Yankee officer on the train with his bacon, the brutes!"

"And they throw his moldy rice after him, teasing that this is his wedding day and he's off on the honeymoon, you see."

"They wanted to enlist me," Seth told them. "Oh, dear boy, don't you let them for a minute!" the door opener gushed. "They got a girl from the neighborhood to riding with them last year, till she fell from the horse and broke a bone in her...buttocks.

Then she came to us, to swear off all that and put her hand into the stream of Eternal Lightning."

With all the pulsing light from the machines, Seth didn't know whether she was only speaking metaphorically. One of the ladies seemed to sense his question: "You can really do that, young man. We have a machine in the next room that can give you just a mild dose of the charge that struck Billy Bunton in the brain that day on the mountain top, altering his mind forever."

"Was he all right? I mean could he still —"

"Better than ever. Re-made his brain in the form of Eternal Scientific Understanding."

"This young lady came here every day to read testimonials with us and put her pretty golden curls in the Eternal Stream. She went away from here with no intention in this world of ever riding that stream bed with those caterwauling brutes again in this earthly life!"

"Thank you, but I don't think I'm up for any more shocks today," Seth told them. "I've had quite a bit of excitement already."

The most motherly of the three said she could understand that and offered him a place in a rocking chair, and a cup of tea, which he accepted.

One of the ladies showed him a sort of testimonial book with color photos of various people with shocked looks on their faces. Beneath were quotes about what they had just experienced from putting their hand in the eternal stream of flowing electrons.

When the tea came, Seth looked about him at the strange scene, and the old ladies in black, sort of cooing around him — as though this was life, and everything raging outside these walls was a kind of insanity — and almost forgot why he had come.

"Do any of you know anything about the history of this house in the 1930s," he asked, his words echoing strangely in the place.

They stared at him, with consternation. But was that from what he had said, or... No, it was the thundering "Blundering Confederates" on horseback, storming by again — that was their concern.

This time "Julia" herself rushed to the window and threw it up: Out of my Dahlias, you brutes!" she screamed, gesturing violently with the teapot. The other two rallied behind her, hurling lady-like curses out the window, but at a volume far below the hearing of the rabid enactors.

There was no talking to these ladies until the cavalry had charged by again, but in the pause that followed Seth re-asked his question.

"Oh, no. This house was built by the local founder of *The Glorious Lightning*. He did not begin construction until the day after Pearl Harbor, and had to finish it by tearing down his former house and using the materials, on account of war shortages.

After the war, he lived upstairs and kept these rooms down here just as you see them, for inviting the blind and down-trodden of all humanity into the stream of Eternal Electron Flow."

Check off another one.

And yet he wouldn't have missed it. Or the adjacent enactors. In its first days, even without Lindsey, this was turning out to be a more interesting vacation than he'd counted on.

But the next couple of days turned out not to be so interesting, and he couldn't reconcile himself to the disappointment of being unable to find the poem-engraved tombstone in the garden behind the house where the old man from the train had once "courted" a girl of Lindsey's age. Maybe it was that the old man had so specifically recommended it to him, as one who had also lost his father early in life.

He tried to put it out of his mind by actually reading the textbooks he had brought home, and by further surfing of history websites in search of term paper ideas. But what the old man had told him had become a small picture of actual history so real in his mind that it drove out mere historical ideas.

On Thursday night he realized that he had overlooked a possibility. With Savannah he had done an Internet search of Edmund street to check for historical references to a street that no longer existed — and found nothing — but he had not done that for Chatham County. He had been too quick to jump when the clerk there had pointed him to the two block Edmund Street in Laurel Dell — and rushed off to check that out. Didn't mean there couldn't have been another Edmund Street back in the 1930's in another County town. And of course the tombstone, with its message prescribed for him, could have survived without the street.

At first the listed hits referred only to the street in Laurel Dell, where he had found only Confederate re-enactors and old ladies keeping the flame of The Glorious Lightning. But buried near the bottom of the hit list was something that lit up the page. The description of a genealogical site — for the "Corbell family" — contained the phrase "and resided for many years on Edmund Street, Chatham County, in the old settlement of Tybee Trace."

When he phoned Chatham County Planning and Zoning again, a clerk told him that the only existing Edmund Street was in Laurel Dell — which he already knew — but that the former settlement of Tybee Trace had been absorbed into the modern suburb of Delta View, not far outside the Savannah City limits. "There might be a few of the original houses near the intersection of Route Seven and Bodley Road. But I can't tell you where any earlier Edmund Street might have been. Could have disappeared when they widened Route Seven to four lanes and a median back in the sixties."

"Thanks. Do you know anyone there who might know what it used to be like?"

The clerk excused himself, and a couple of minutes later a different man came on the phone, and said he knew an old lady in a nursing home, a friend of his grandmother, who had lived in Tybee Trace. "Still got her head about her. She might could tell you how it was."

Seth took down her name and that of the nursing home.

His mother was off that Friday but had needed the car, so he had to wait until she returned in late afternoon before driving out to the Angels Rest Home. Mrs. Maud Pembrau was a feeble old lady in a wheelchair, getting ready to go to dinner, but when he named the man at the County building who had mentioned her, she smiled and said she "remembered him well" and could "wait a little to eat."

Yes, she had known Tybee Trace as a girl and young woman. Her best friend, Ginny, had lived there with her parents and two younger brothers.

"Do you remember a house on an Edmund Street with a shaded rear garden?"

"Well, I believe there were several like that. The one I knew — back in the Depression times — where

Ginny's family lived, was on the corner with Oak Road. Number 1100 Edmund — spent many a happy time there in my late teens."

Without looking, Seth sank down onto a chair. Only it was not a chair but a magazine rack, which – collapsing – floored him.

He scrambled up, apologizing — absurdly, to the rack itself. But Mrs. Maud Pembrau seemed not to have noticed, so rapt was she with the memory of 1100 Edmund: "Remember it well. There was a little old burial ground from long before in that rear garden, but that didn't stop Ginny's family from forever holding parties there. I met my future husband at one of them. But Ginny, very popular girl who had many beaus — it was there she lost the one she cared about the most." She sighed long. "The young can be so … They take hurts all so serious. I can't remember what happened between them — everyone had been drinking too much, and it was late. But I know it didn't seem to me such a big thing even then that it couldn't have been patched up. But that young man want back up north where he lived, and she never saw him anymore."

"Do you remember his name?"

"Well…I almost can. I believe there was a pet name she had for him, and if I could recall that…"

"Do you remember a large gravestone at that burial site that had a poem carved into it?"

She was shaking her head. "That doesn't ring any bell with me. But I guess as a young girl I wasn't real interested in tombstones."

"Is the house still there?"

"Last I heard. They took down some of the Tybee Trace houses to widen Route Seven, but not old 1100."

Seth got her to promise to give him a couple of more minutes before going off to dinner, and ran out to the car to get his map. The old girl was good — had to hold it up close to her face to read, but she pointed quickly to the spot of the old house, now off a service road to Route Seven.

"How can you be so sure of the location?" he asked her. "I mean with no more Edmunds, and no Oak Road either for reference?"

She smiled and stared off. "Before I had to move in here, I went there to see it one more time. It was then I saw where it was with the streets of today."

Seth felt like hugging her, but didn't know how she'd take it, and he was in such a hurry now to get to the old house.

He offered to push her to dinner, and she accepted. He had thanked her and started down the hall, when he heard her voice calling: "Young man, young man — I just remembered that boy's name!"

He returned to her table, her face beaming now. "At first I re-called "bear" — I knew that was part of it. Then it came to me: Ginny called him her "Teddy Bear". Because his first name was Ted — I'm sure of that!"

Once in the car, Seth forced himself to focus and breathe before starting off. There was no question now — that had been the first name the old man had told them on the train but he had not been able to remember.

He estimated it as maybe a fifteen-minute drive from the Angels' Rest Home to the site Mrs. Pembrau had indicated on his map. But now, driving the back roads there and so close to his goal, his thoughts migrated away from finding the father poem on the tombstone and to the last years with his own father.

During the early teenage years there had been confrontations with him over authority — probably pretty common stuff, he thought now, but at the time it had seemed earth shaking and bitter. At that point he had pictured the man as an inflexible, out-of-touch old tyrant, but that had gradually eased. And a big change occurred when he had gone off to college. His father must have made a conscious decision to treat him more like a man. Then when he had been diagnosed with the cancer, that had made a huge difference. He didn't lay down the law anymore, and proclamations to his son mainly gave way to questions for his son — real ones.

He had returned to religion, abandoned in his twenties. At first, Seth had thought, *Oh, the old standard thing — now that he's afraid of dying, he wants to get right with Heaven. Just in case there is one – the prudent insurance policy.*

But he would come to see that it went much deeper. In the last months of his life, his father had interpreted a scripture passage after supper in the kitchen — to the effect that the withering away of self-concepts was the necessary precondition for the experience of God. Only then was the self "up for eternity." He would not have thought his father capable of such a thought, but what impressed him more was how you could see that idea taking actual shape in him: the old stubbornness and self-defenses dropping away and making him so much more available to his wife and son — and everyone.

Seth even went to church with him a couple of times toward the end, and the last time something happened that he would not forget. His dad was in a wheelchair by then, and the two of them were in the center aisle opposite the last pew to the rear. At a certain point in the service a middle aged woman was there beside them, marshaling a children's choir — getting the kids of maybe eight or nine ready to process forward to sing their song. She told them to take out their hymn sheets and have them ready. There was a great deal or reaching under vestments into pockets and bringing out of song sheets, and the choir director was checking that each child had one. When she came to the smallest boy, she asked where his music was. Seth and his father had turned around, watching the little drama, and he had been surprised to see that the boy was gripping a Transformer — a non-electronic toy that had been out of date even when he was that age, as fun as it had been to turn a jet plane into a super hero, say, just by moving mechanical parts.

"Bucky, that's just a toy!" hissed the children's choir director. "Where's your music!"

The little boy mounted his defense quickly:

"Yeah, but it's a Transformer!"

At that his dad had begun to chuckle. In a moment that turned into a chortling too loud to suppress, and he had motioned Seth to wheel him out into the vestibule where he could let it loose without disturbing others. Out there, he had laughed to the bottom of his heart, and it still seemed to Seth that had been some kind of happy, near final letting go of life for him. Two days later he was dead.

And if he hadn't turned into such a different character in his last years, I wouldn't miss him so.

It was twilight when he reached the point on his map so confidently indicated by Mrs. Maud Pembrau. Wouldn't it have been interesting, he suddenly thought, if Mr. Ted whatever-last-name had gotten off that train in Savannah, and he had been able to get him together here with Mrs. Maud. Both seemed to have excellent memories despite their age — together, they could have revisited intense scenes from seventy years before, back when they were his own age, cleared up old mysteries and misunderstandings perhaps, and stared in wonder at their two selves, then and now.

And there, fifty yards away, was the house of Mr. Ted's 1930's courtship! It was boarded-up and ruinous, but behind: the tree shaded garden the old man had spoken of.

And now his heart really did begin to hammer. He approached the mounded area — the possible burial ground. There was no standing tombstone, but would it be there fallen to the ground with its father poem intact?

Seth stopped and stared at the mass of vines and over-grown weeds, and saw no stone.

It was only as he moved forward, still seeing nothing in the tangled brush beneath, that he suddenly stumbled, looked down and realized that he had tripped on the raised edge of a large stone.

Once he realized the size of it and saw its shape sunk deep into the earth, he despaired of ever turning it over to read the inscription. Nothing short of two men with crowbars could do that. And how much of any carved text could have survived decades buried in damp ground?

It was then he saw two English letters — there, right under the heel of his hand!

It's fallen on its back — no Bugs Bunny poster, this one!

In seconds he had ripped away the vines and used his hands and forearms to rake the surface clean enough to read.

The title, carved in larger font, was clear: *What Father Now?*

Beneath, the smaller font of the poem's text — perhaps carved less deeply — was severely eroded, and much was missing. With pain he saw how much was gone.

This human effort at truth had proved too frail and been worn away. Eroded back into the old rough blind stone beneath his fingers. Suddenly weeping, he sat hunched over, trying to decipher what remained to speak to him.

Two or three short phrases were clear, a word or a couple of letters here and there, but that was all.

At some point the non-sequential phrases, not really making sense together, did begin to speak — in the way gibberish can when the need for meaning is enough. Touching for what was there and heartbreaking for what was missing.

He took out the small history notebook he had carried through all this and began to make a copy of what could still be read:

What Father Now?

....

....

.... *the very breath for breathin*

....

So strange et close..

....

Grander view............................*of*..... *father*

Never seen but .... *of*........ *eart.*

It was getting dark, and his mom would expect him home. He put the notebook in his side pocket and returned to the car.

On the drive back into Savannah, he first turned on the radio. But soon there were other words sounding in his head.

*So strange yet (*it must have been) *close*.... He turned off the radio. *The grander view...of father... never seen but ...*

Never seen but what?

Mr. Ted Whoever had not been able to give him everything he had hoped — time had eroded most of it away. But that short note secretly placed in his shoulder bag pocket had led on and led on... to this that he was so glad to have even in its haunting incompleteness.

As he turned into his street, the cell phone began ringing.

"Hey boy, we're back. Where you been all afternoon?"

"Great."

"Unless you've already lined up several other chicks, I could go out soon."

"Good. I'm almost home. I'll swing by for you in an hour plus."

"Okay. If you could make it by 7:15, there's a movie I've heard is good at the—"

"Let's do that tomorrow, Lindsey. Tonight I'd like to talk to you someplace quiet. Maybe just park somewhere."

"And all you want to do is talk!"

"For a while. I've got some pretty wonderful stuff to tell you. Not sure if I should tell my mom."

"Just teasing you, boy. I'm always up for wonderful."

Chapter Six:
Learning After School

This is like, working perfect, Joanie thought. *Miss Carol is doing such a super job agreeing with the mom, alias Darthie Vader, on my character flaws that the mom actually approves of her!*

And that meant that she could go over to Miss Carol's house and furniture restoration shop after school on lots of afternoons without getting in trouble — now that she'd learned which bus would get her home on time to her mom's fancy new condo on the harbor.

Those afternoons, when she wasn't talking to Miss Carol or helping her out in the shop, she was down in the basement of her house going through the boxes of things Uncle Ted had left behind. This was where she had discovered his wife's wedding ring in an envelope and his beautiful note leaving it to her, but now it was slow going. Sometimes she would have to read through papers of his notes many times and put them together with others near them to have any idea what they were about. Talk about studying — school was nothing compared to this. But this was different because she didn't love those historical characters in textbooks, not like this one who had stepped off into history only six months ago.

"You learning much about your uncle from all that time down there?" Miss Carol asked her one afternoon.

"Now I think I am, from diary-type stuff he left. Never realized how much he loved tutoring those kids at Dudley Elementary and Middle. For twenty years. Then something happened. I don't think they kicked him out because he was too old or anything, but it was like he just decided he couldn't do it anymore. Which made him very sad."

"That *is* sad."

"And you remember what Mom Darthie heard from the Florida police and we learned more about at the funeral — that about his giving stuff away right up to his heart attack at home plate of the spring training game in Florida?

"Let's see," Miss Carol said. "It was the meals he bought on the train for people, and also giving away his sleeper bed to a young mom whose baby couldn't sleep in the coach. And was there a huge tip to the porter when he left the train?"

"Correct, and don't forget all the hundred dollar bills he gave away at home plate. Before he couldn't anymore."

"I'll never forget that." Miss Carol said.

"Now I think I'm starting to get what he was up to there. But not my mom!" Joanie suddenly felt herself shift into mad: "You know what Darthie Vader thinks his reason was? She said it was to spend as much as possible to keep it away from her. *Her.* That's how she thinks — everything is done related to *her.* But you know in his will — which she's had a copy of for a long time — he left everything remaining to *me.* And I know my Uncle Ted would not have given away money to keep it from me."

"No, he wouldn't."

"So really, it was like he had come to the time in his life ... He couldn't do the school tutoring anymore, and he knew Darthie was set to stick him in a gross nursing home..."

"And?"

"I think for him it was like, 'time is short, so everything in life has changed.' And that sleeper room and money was what he had left to give away, plus that personal something he was always trying to give people."

"Yes," Miss Carol said. "And which they wouldn't always take. But he was lucky to have you as his niece — who would."

Joanie felt the tears at that. She should have had a mom like this who was slender and pretty, could do craft stuff and — most of all — understood people in their hearts. She thanked her now and said goodbye and took the bus home. But from that afternoon — having put all that together — some plan was working in her head. Just a matter of time before it came clear.

Because it was money he had given *her*. It was hers to do something true with, like he had.

That was why three days later she did not catch the bus home from school, or walk to Miss Carols, but headed off down the sidewalk in the opposite direction, toward the inner city.

That school had let out by the time she got there, so not many people were around, and she just walked right into the building with no questions asked and went straight to the principal's office.

The secretary gave her a disrespectful look, Joanie thought. Who was *she*, the look said — just a teenager, with heart patches over the knees of her jeans. "I'd like to talk to the principal," she told the woman. "On like, important business."

"Oh, really. Do you have an appointment?" Now she was looking contempt at the little good luck doll Joanie had tied into her ponytail.

"Negative. But money talks." She left the sec to figure out what she meant by that.

The woman jerked her big piled-up hairdo away so fast toward her magazine that Joanie thought she was lucky not to have got the whiplash.

"I can hear she's got someone in there now, so I'll wait, but is there anything else I need to do to get in and see her?

This stuck-up sec gave her a complete up and down stare-over. "She's a busy woman, leaving here after she's done with that parent conference."

"Okay. Just give me a time I can come back for an appointment."

"For what purpose?"

'That's what I want to discuss with her."

"Don't play games with me! This ain't your school. Get back to your own school and talk to your own principal."

"It's not about that. The principal here is a certified public employee. My mom pays like, taxes and fees toward her upkeep. I mean her salary. I just want to talk to her a couple of minutes. Not asking for some kind of audience with the Pope."

"Now you watch your language, Miss—"

Just then the door opened, and here was a wide-tailed woman of about her mom's age, leading out a slender girl whom Joanie thought looked only a few years older than she was. This large principal in the bright red dress leaned over the young parent to open the outer door, so that her widest part pointed at Joanie like some flaming emergency signal.

That red butt, straight at me, Joanie thought. *A warning, because I can hear already how she talks that slow, slow reasoning full of rules and restrictions, which to cut through I'll have to go fast and jazzy.*

"Could I have seventeen seconds with you?" she asked the Principal.

The woman was tall as well as broad, and she looked straight down at her over the tops of her glasses: "Actually, as I'm sure Mrs. Glutz has told you, pre-approved appointments in this office are a necessary requirement, and the actual granting of all appointments is purpose-driven."

"That's wildly beyond reproach!" Joanie cried. "And my purpose is to continue the tutoring my great uncle Ted Costas did here for twenty years and support it with a donation of actual dollars."

"Due to budget constraints, that tutoring program has been retroactively de-funded. And of a certainty it would take more than the donation of a few dollars to reconstitute it, with all possible revisions, and orchestrate a time table for bringing it back on line."

"Not talking a few dollars," Joanie said. "How does thirty thousand of those suckers sound to you?"

"Perhaps you'd better come inside," the Principal said.

Once in her office, she told Joanie to take the chair opposite her. "We appreciated your uncle's work here," she said. "But I believe he decided some months ago to portray his talents elsewhere."

"Like in heaven. He died in March."

"Oh. My condolences."

"Thanks."

"The amount of money you mentioned could compensate one of our administrators for her time in re-starting and then supervising the volunteer tutoring program. For — I would offer as my best estimate — two years. Of course, a differentially greater amount might endow the program to some distant future point in time."

"That's half of what I'm inheriting. I think I should keep the other half for needs that might come up."

"May I ask your age?"

"I'm fifteen."

The Principal pressed her lips together and nodded a couple of times. "I believe as a minor there may be constraints on how you spend the funds from that inheritance."

"What do you mean — it was left to me in the will!"

"Truly, but your parent or legal guardian may have to approve the allocation of that inherited funding. Until you yourself reach age eighteen."

Soon after, Joanie stood up to leave. "What you told me — it's maybe right, and I'm all shook up now."

"Sorry, dear. Just carrying out my duty to report all possible constraints. If your parent or legal guardian agrees with your spending plan, I would assume there would be no major difficulty with proceeding toward re-activation and implementation of that program. Let me know."

All the way home, walking and then on the bus, this burned in her. She confronted her mom at dinner over stuffed peppers. They had been brought from the deli in the basement of the condo — Darthie thought that was a cool thing to do now that she was rich — and she was setting them down on the table in the same plastic microwaveable tray they had come in. In the center of the two green peppers the round hamburger and ketchup tops were sizzling and hissing like angry blood-shot eyes at Joanie, as she went right to it: "What if I want to spend some of the money Uncle Ted left me in the will. Spend it now?"

"The will is still in probate."

"For how long?"

"Maybe a couple of more weeks, if we're lucky."

"The 'we're' — why would that make *you* lucky too?"

The mom cleared her throat. "For now, we need that money as a family. I've told you it makes sense to purchase this condo, which we are only renting now. But — at least until the Orioles settlement is complete — we'll need that Ted Costas money toward the purchase."

Joanie put down her fork. "For how long? When do I get to spend the money he left me?"

"We *will be* spending it — some, I can't say now exactly how much, as a contribution to the cost of this new home."

"Wait a government-certified minute here! So really it's not just 'for now'! You're actually saying that part of my gift from Uncle Ted is going away forever. But I never said I wanted to move to this place! The Crossley Street apartment was fine for me. You did this for you. Where do you get the right to spend my Uncle Ted money that I don't for one second approve!"

"Calm down, Joanie. You are a minor child in this family. You are not a single adult. It's entirely legal — you can call my lawyer if you don't believe me — to spend part of the money you will inherit for the living space that you too will benefit from. Think of it as your share, your contribution to the cost of our housing."

Joanie jumped up from the table, because she couldn't sit still for this: "That's like taxation on me that I never agreed to. We just studied that in history — it's 'taxation without representation'!"

"Think how you benefit from living in a better class set-up like—"

"I'm calling the lawyer. This is robbery — I can't believe it's legal."

Darthie Vader rolled her eyes, but she gave his phone number. Not a good sign, Joanie thought. Must mean she really had already checked this out to be sure he would support her.

The man talked smarter than the Principal, but he had that same style of using as many words as possible to say the simplest thing.

"Excuse me, but you're saying I got no choice? As long as I might possibly benefit in any imaginary way from living in this fancy dump, I got to let her take a big hunk of what Uncle Ted left me for that?"

A couple of million syllables later, it turned out that yes, that was what he was saying.

"Well, let me ask you this. Since as my mom, she buys me things that benefit me all the time, what's to stop her from charging me for all that too, as soon as I get this so-called inheritance of mine? She like buys me tooth paste to use, and I guess it's a benefit that my teeth don't rot and fall out, so why not take all that and dentist bills too from my so- called inheritance? But wait — it's to my benefit to eat, and I don't eat as much as her, but she could like charge me like forty percent of all the grocery and deli bills."

"Well actually, you make —"

"And why not charge me for my drugstore supplies that I need now of a personal female nature because it's to my benefit not to —"

"Joanie Rudgear, you watch your language, or you'll end up grounded and wishing you weren't!"

"Joanie, you actually make a possible point there," the lawyer said now. "That's probably a gray area in the law, where the ordinary responsibilities of parent for child support might not be appropriate for the use of such an inheritance. But when it comes to more expensive and major benefits, like the place you both live, in the absence of any directives from your uncle, or even statement of his wishes...."

"I understand," Joanie said, quieter because she really wasn't mad at the lawyer. "Without Uncle Ted having written anything about that, she gets to be a certified, swirling-around-with-her-big-purse kind of woman dictator. Look alike for King George the Third with her taxation without representation — or maybe Joseph Stalin himself in reincarnation!"

She didn't sleep but tossed in bed for at least two hours that night, before coming to a plan. Only when the excitement wore down, did she begin to breathe heavy and escape from it all.

"You're a big camper, right?" she said to Caster Hedges the next day after school. "You've got all that stuff at home, and you're my so-called boyfriend, so what's the problem with your helping me out here?"

"Okay then. I guess we could do it."

After they finished setting up the stuff in the hall outside the door of the mom's condo, Caster left, and there she was. But this was no good — the mom had to know she was here to have an effect. Joanie let herself into the apartment with her key on pretext of using the bathroom.

"Oh, you're here," the mom said, after she flushed the toilet to get her attention. "We eat in an hour. Where you going?"

"To my new room," Joanie said and went out into the hall, slamming the door loud enough that she would get it.

She had just time enough to duck in under the tent, and push the end of Caster's sleeping bag further out into the hall so no one could miss it, before the mom opened the door and came looking for her.

"What are you *doing*!" she exploded — at the level of upset that Joanie had hoped for.

"Camping out here. That apartment belongs to you. I don't live there, so I don't get any benefit from it."

For once, the mom was wordless. Now Joanie couldn't resist sticking her head out of the tent far enough to see her face. What Darthie was staring at was the clothesline that Caster had helped rig from the top of the tent pole to the fire extinguisher. What was likely causing her mouth to hang open like in a horror movie was the sight of her pajamas for tonight and underclothes for tomorrow hanging there.

After breathing hard, she broke into words:

"This is a high class building. What will our neighbors think of us when they see this!"

"I couldn't guess," Joanie said. "That's up to them."

It didn't take long to find out. Within a few minutes the single woman and then the couple who lived further down their hall passed by silently with looks of extreme distaste, pressing close to the opposite wall, as though the tent might have been set down here directly by heliocopter from some jungle full of tropical diseases. The mom slunk back into her unit, wordless.

In the next hour a parade of people from other floors came to view the campsite and whisper. Joanie emerged from the tent and tried smiling and helloing to invite a conversation, but none of them would speak to her. One did ask another, clearly for her benefit, "Can you believe she'd be allowed to do that?"

Then the night manager arrived. He did not speak to Joanie, but rang the bell to the apartment. A frazzled looking mom answered him that it was "just a trial of the camping equipment. For one night only. It will all be down tomorrow morning."

This was something Joanie hadn't thought of: the mom was upset enough to totally transform into her Darthie Vader self, and the minute she left for school in the morning throw Caster's stuff in the dumpster, or put it in her new SUV and drive it to the landfill.

And she couldn't protect it by carrying it along to school to stash somewhere — too bulky and heavy.

"Just a government-certified minute here!"

She called to the night manager, who was starting to walk away. Now was the time to rev up the pressure, before the mom could maybe take all this away in the morning. "No one night stand here, Mr. Manager. This is now my place to camp out, week after week, outside my mom's door. I'm not going to be living anymore in the apartment."

"Don't listen to her," Darthie said. "This is just a prank."

"Tomorrow morning," the Night Manager said. "Mrs. Ridschnick comes in at nine a.m. If this is still here, she will take care of the situation."

He walked off, but Joanie turned to the tense, flustered face of the mom: "And I mean it too. If you take this stuff away — which is Caster's, so you'd have to pay him back — I'll just take my PJs, a blanket and pillow from inside and sleep out here with that. And hang my bra and panties for the next day right on that fire extinguisher."

Again, the mom said nothing. She just shook her head as though in a daze and went back into the apartment.

Joanie surprised herself by getting a pretty good night's sleep in the tent. The sleeping bag was cozy, and by ten o'clock the overhead lights were auto-dimmed, and no one walked the hall. She knew it might be different on a weekend night — people coming back late from partying could make sleeping rough, but maybe by then the mom would agree to something.

Around seven-thirty in the morning, just as she was coming out of the bathroom in the apartment, the mom called to her in a different zombie voice: "Joanie, please come have your orange juice and cereal here. I want to discuss this."

Turned out she was actually ready to offer like a peace treaty. Not like the Yorktown peace, because she was not surrendering. She still wanted to take half her Uncle Ted inheritance to help buy this apartment, but would put the other half in a bank account for Joanie to spend as she wanted.

"I'll take it," she said.

"You will?" The mom looked surprised.

"Yeah, I've been reading where Uncle Ted wrote that money was not something to fight over but to give to people."

"Maybe when you're about to die. For the rest of us it's to build up and keep safe. Where have you been reading that from your uncle?"

Woops. Maybe a big mistake for my seeing Miss Carol!

"Oh, a few things he left me. No big thing."

The mom lost interest and let it drop. Good thing she had never told her about finding the ring at Miss Carol's but had kept it hidden. And if she ever learned how close Miss Carol felt to Uncle Ted, that would be disaster.

That day after school she found out some of the reason for the mom's quick peace offer.

"She phoned me last night," Miss Carol told her. "Soon after the scene with the condo night manager in the hall. She called me for advice on what to do."

"Wow and double wow! Shows what a great job you're doing with her of slamming my character flaws!"

Miss Carol smiled. "That must have been quite a scene with your underclothes on the line from the tent, and the horrified neighbors checking it out. But when your mom called asking me what action she could take to make you give that up and come inside like any normal respectable girl, I did my best to picture extreme effects on the neighbors of a fight with the apartment management, or child welfare workers called in, police called in."

"Good job!"

"She could see that would just make her look less respectable in the building. Which she cares about to a rather sad degree."

"Yeah, for sure."

"Joan, you see how that's fear and insecurity in her? When you consider that, she's not such a Darthie Vader."

"Yeah, I guess that's true psychology," Joanie said.

"It's also religious compassion, which helps us understand someone else by taking a larger view of what we all are."

It was a couple of days later that Miss Carol talked to her about Uncle Ted and his jingles and slogans. She had known he wasn't proud of them, but never why. "He felt it was adding to the lies of big advertising," Miss Carol explained. "And that was 'poisoning the world', he told me."

"Really? I think advertising is just like ... dumb and obvious. Like cheerleaders, our team is the best —'Rah, Rah, Rah'. Not serious stuff."

"True, but that's not the kind that bothered him. It's where it manipulates peoples' self-doubts and fears. Confirms their prejudices and hatreds. Or plain deceives them out of their money."

"Yeah, like what?"

"Well. You know my daughter Sarah is off at college in her freshman year. Let me show you what she got in the mail." She rose and went over to the shelf above the kitchen table, and brought back the envelope. "Sarah's lucky Larry and I got through to her about credit cards, so she mailed this home for us to check. You see what it says in the big print?"

"'HOW ABOUT AN INTEREST FREE CREDIT CARD!'", Joanie read.

"Sounds great, right? Also, see what it says there about 'Use these checks and write yourself an interest free loan – treat yourself to some of the luxuries you deserve!'"?

"Yep."

"Now turn it over and read what it says in these tiny letters at the bottom of the page."

Joanie gave it a shot, but then gave it up. "I don't understand a lot of those words, like 'residual outstanding balance' and 'promotional rate with limited special application to eligible transactions', 'restricted to sixty days from initial posting' and junk like that."

"Of course, you don't. And that's what they count on — that most of their customers won't. See that number there?"

"Nineteen percent?"

"They advertise that it's "interest free", but that's what the interest rate goes to on any items not paid for within the sixty days. Most people don't pay off most of their card debt within the month, and the banks know most won't pay much off within two months. So the nineteen is what they'll soon be paying on most of their charges. And I'm guessing you, or my college freshman, or lots of other people have no idea what banks are *paying out* to their savings customers right now."

Joanie shook her head.

"About a quarter of one percent. That's current at the one offering this card, American Heritage Bank. I checked. A little more if you lock your money up with them for one to five years and don't take anything out."

"Wow. How is that fair?"

"It gets worse. If you miss a monthly payment even once, then the new interest rate goes to thirty percent. And then if you start to pay it back, they work it so the charges at thirty percent are paid off last. Same deal if Sarah used any of those 'free checks' they so kindly mailed her."

"Wow and double wow."

"That's one example of why your Uncle Ted felt bad about his career in advertising, though he was valued as a slogan and jingle-writing genius."

Joanie said very little the rest of the afternoon, but she was putting this new info together with some of her great uncle's little notes that she had been reading through downstairs. By the time she got on the bus to go home, she could again feel a plan beginning to form.

Around nine o'clock that night when the mom was safely distracted by a favorite TV program, she called Caster from her bedroom. "I got another protest for us," she announced.

Was that a little groan that he'd tried to hold down?

"I need you to help me with it in art class tomorrow afternoon and right after, but this time you won't have to lend me anything."

Being a sort of scaredy cat, he wasn't enthusiastic once she explained it to him, but he was a good writer, which was needed for this. And she talked him up for that.

In the art studio she did the front of the poster in big bold lettering, and he did the back, where there was more writing, to explain it all.

"Cover it up!" he hissed the minute the teacher, Mrs. Lessier came back into the studio. "If she sees it, she'll never let it out of here!"

That was probably true, Joanie thought. This so-called boy friend did have his points.

School was out at three, and by three-fifteen the two of them were standing in front of the American Heritage Bank branch on nearby Brownlow Avenue. Each held one end of the big poster board sign with the bright red lettering:

American Heritage Bank Says,
"How About An Interest-Free Credit Card?"
We the people answer,
"How About Telling Us The Truth?"
(See reverse side for the truth!)

From the moment they set up, a good number of people would pause to read the front of the sign, and maybe half of those would go around back to read the explanation of how the offer was basically a lie, meant to hook customers into high interest — for life, if possible. And then some of those would take the one page handout that explained the same thing.

"A lot are stopping to read," Caster said. "I'm surprised."

Just a minute after he said that, a bank security guard waddled up to them, looked at the front of the poster, but did not bother to go around back. "You're trespassing," he told them. "You need to get off bank property."

"Then where does the public sidewalk begin?" Joanie demanded.

The man — his badge said "Bertram"— shook his head, annoyed.

"Come forward three steps," she said to Caster. "Now I *know* we're on public sidewalk. We got a right to assemble in public and 'petition for the... What's that word in the Constitution, Caster?"

The so-called boyfriend shook his head.

"Whatever, we're here to 'petition for the blankety blank of grievances," she told the security guard. "We're now on public property, and we've got a grievance against this bank."

Bertram made a round of his lips, like he was about to whistle, but he just turned and walked deliberately away, fingering his billy club.

She and Caster were both encouraged when a middle aged man and then two old ladies stopped to congratulate them. They read the back of the poster and picked up some of the handout pages and began offering them to those passing by. "The banks have been getting away with this for years," one of the old ladies said. "It's time someone blew the whistle, and right on their front porch!"

"Bless you kids," the man said. "For what you're doing."

Joanie thanked them, but a minute later a big tough policeman swaggered up to them, and she thought *woops, this might be the end of it!*

"Mr. Police," she cried, "we don't mean to break any law — we're just using our constitutional right to petition for the blankety-blank of grievances!"

"Watch your language, dear," one of the old ladies said. "Profanity only hurts the cause."

"Oh, it's just that word I can't think of," Joanie said. "It means like, 'blow those grievances into outer space forever'."

" 'Redress!' Caster cried. "That's the word!"

"Right!" Joanie said. "We want to redress the heck out of those suckers!"

"All that's okay, kids." The big policeman actually seemed cool about it. "Just move over a little to the left by the wall there, so as not to interfere with the traffic in and out of the bank."

"That's wildly beyond reproach!" Joanie told him. "We can do that."

"You can protest on a public sidewalk. As long as you keep it decent and don't create a public nuisance."

The policeman actually stayed to read the back of the poster board and walked away with one of the handouts.

While he was there, he drew a crowd — maybe people were expecting an arrest or something. But after he left, many stayed to read the material and talk. One man shouted angrily at them — something about being "red", it sounded like — but most people told them they were doing a good thing.

"We're reaching a lot of people here," Caster marveled.

Not long after a TV truck arrived from a local channel. A well-dressed young woman asked if she could interview them, and Joanie said, "Naturally. We want everyone to know about this and not get ripped off!"

Toward the end of the interview, Joanie was asked why she personally had taken this on. She hesitated a couple of seconds, and then it came to her: "My great uncle, who is dead now, was sorry he had made money from the lies of advertising. He wrote, not long before he died, "How can we ever live together in truth if the Big Money Boys are always lying to us?"

"Thank you, Joan Rudgear, age fifteen. At the American Heritage Bank in South Brownlow, I'm Christine Flowers, for Live Wire News."

"Wow and double wow," Joanie said to Caster. "I was on TV. Where's our sign?"

Where indeed was the poster they had made in art class, which had drawn such favorable reviews? It seemed to have disappeared. They asked around among the crowd of folks who had stayed to listen to the interview, and two people said that a bank security guard had picked it up where they had left it leaning against the front wall of the building and taken it away.

"Figures. Like Uncle Ted would say, that's the crooked Big Money boys for you."

When she got home, Joanie found that the mom had happened to see the TV interview. She gave her a couple of warnings about getting in trouble with banks and police, but — surprisingly — seemed a little proud of her.

But the next afternoon at Miss Carol's she found something in one of the boxes of Uncle Ted leavings that blew all that out of her head. Picking through typical pages of old letters received, receipts, hand-written notes and small notebooks with assorted thoughts, she came across something that looked more official: here in large envelope was a page he had bothered to print out, including his name at the bottom. The heading was

Last Will and Testament
of Theodore Paul Costas

Written by me, March 21, 2009, to cancel all my
previous wills.

"Wow, written a week before he died," she said aloud. "Maybe just before Darthie put him in the hospital for tests." But what would it say?

It was not hard to find out. The will was less than a page. It said that he left all his furniture to his nephew's widow, Mrs. Robyn Brawnley Rudgear, and all his books and all his money — investments and cash— to her daughter, his great niece Miss Joan Ann Rudgear. The money was to be used for one purpose only, and that was for Joan Ann Rudgear's college education — and if any was left, for her graduate school education — and the spending of that money was to be under the strict supervision of Mr. Gregor Galineades, Attorney at Law, of Baltimore, MD. The choice of colleges/universities and related decisions were to be made by Miss Joan Ann Rudgear, in consultation with Mr. Gregor Galineades.

Joanie leaned back. She had never thought much about going to college one way or the other, but this was like a word coming from beyond. It came straight from her dear Uncle Ted, who — though passed on — was directing her footsteps on the path of life. She was all teared up. Now she wanted to do college.

Miss Carol was really happy about it, and suggested she make a copy on the machine in the furniture restoration office and leave it with her for safe keeping.

This is working out perfect, Joanie thought when she got home and heard they were eating early because the mom's lawyer, that Mr. Judson, was coming over to finalize some things about the Hopkins settlement.

"I'd like us both to talk to him for a minute first," Joanie said.

When Judson arrived, bright-eyed at their door, the first words out of his mouth were, "I hear you and your mom came to a compromise on the use of your inheritance in the will. That's good. Very sensible."

"I guess," Joanie answered. "But any way, that's now history. This is what matters." And she pulled out the new will and handed it to the lawyer.

The mom was reading over his shoulder, her face working itself into a dark Darthie scowl. "How can I raise this child to age eighteen for any college — not to mention expenses when she's home in summers — with no help from that money he left. It's not fair!"

"I think you'll be in plenty good shape, thanks to Hopkins and the Orioles," Judson said with a tired look. "But you needn't worry — this paper doesn't change anything."

"Why not? It's what my uncle wanted done with his money!"

This lawyer actually looked sympathetic to her, Joanie thought. "You're probably right. Unfortunately, it won't stand up in court. He made a common mistake of folks who draw up their own wills. This entire document looks like it was done in Times New Roman, twelve point, probably in Microsoft Word, and that is hardly distinctive and recognizable as a product of Mr. Ted Costas. I'm not denying that he wrote it, but from a legal standpoint, anyone might have written it."

"You mean if he had just done it in his handwriting ..."

"Right. At least his signature. Assuming that there are still people who could attest to the signature as his."

"Joanie, you don't need college anyway. You just need to be smart about money, and I can teach you that."

But she wasn't listening, being too busy trying to picture whether near the bottom of that dusty box there might have been a hand-written copy of this same later Will. She had grabbed the envelope with its printed page as seeming more official, but just maybe...

Sleep was hard that night. She had been satisfied enough with the deal of splitting her inheritance with the mom, and there was even something appealing about having half the money right away and not having it all held for college in the future, but none of that seemed to matter in her heart now. Her Uncle had liked to read, liked to think on his own about things, and he had wanted that for her. He had willed to her his books, and college. Coming late, six months after his death — it was a voice from heaven, like. Taking hold of her with sure hands. That made her cry again.

The next day after school Miss Carol went with her down to the basement room where the boxes were. They found it together — just as she had half-remembered: the hand written version, clearly readable, had been just below the printed one in the envelope. They took it carefully to the furniture restoration office and made copies.

Miss Carol said that she could testify that this was his handwriting — she had seen it many times. Shortly after her husband Larry arrived home and pointed out that since the will was still in probate,

Uncle Ted's money would still be in bank or brokerage accounts, which would likely have his signature on file, so they would be able to attest to it as well. They were both so excited that they offered to drive her to see the lawyer, Judson, before he left his office for the afternoon.

It turned out the mom's lawyer looked pleased that there was now a version of the new will that, as he said, "ought to pass muster".

"Do you know this lawyer, Galineades?" he asked her.

"Oh, yeah — he's a nice man. I met him at Uncle Ted's a couple of times. From his church. I think he'll be good on how to do college."

The lawyer hesitated. "He's not as old as your uncle was?"

"No. My mom's age."

"Excellent. But let's see if we can get him on the phone. Maybe he doesn't know about this."

It turned out that he did know, but hadn't known until recently. "Ted spoke to me informally about it one day at church some months before his death, but not having heard anything further, I thought he must have changed his mind. Actually, he had mailed a letter about it to my office, but it had been misfiled until earlier this week, for which I sincerely apologize. And I will be very happy to work with Joan when the time comes."

The mom was *not* very happy when Joanie explained it to her that night. She called the lawyer to make sure it was true, with no way out of it. She looked tired and went to bed early.

But the next morning at breakfast, she seemed better.

"I'm sorry if this makes it harder for you to buy this place instead of renting," Joanie told her.

"Uh, probably not. The Hopkins settlement payment is expected this week, and I think we'll be okay to buy it then."

"Cool. I'm starting to get okay with living here. Since my camping out night, some of the neighbors look at me funny, but I'm starting to like the view from the windows. Gives me a feeling of the big picture, the world like stretched out there waiting for something good to be done in it."

"Glad you're starting to appreciate it." The mom paused, looking calmer, less like Darthie Vader than in a while. "And it's not like we don't get anything out of that money going for college. Even if you don't get a better job that way, it'll sound good to say you're away at college."

The next day at Miss Carol's Joanie said, "You see, that's all Uncle Ted's caring about my education is to her."

This older woman she had come to trust nodded in that thoughtful way, studying her face. "That same outlook used to get to your uncle. He came to believe that it was not just companies that distorted with advertising claims, but all of us personally. So for her, your going to college means she gets to have a new line in the advertisements of herself."

"But why does she have to be so into that?"

"We're all of us hungry, but your mom is starving." Miss Carol hesitated, like she didn't know whether to say more. "Of course, she doesn't know it, and couldn't accept it, so I'm trying to hand feed her, a bit at a time." She took a deep breath, and her face lightened. "But she is coming around some. Told me something yesterday I've been saving up for you."

At that point she offered juice and cookies, which Joanie as usual did not turn down. She got a cup of tea for herself and sat opposite her at the kitchen table, more formal than usual — like this was going to be something big, Joanie thought.

"A strange man phoned me yesterday," she began. "But he didn't stay strange for long. A doctor, a cancer specialist from Pikesville, and he was at that Florida spring training game and saw your Uncle Ted die."

Joanie set down her juice glass very carefully on the table.

"But I'm skipping ahead. The reason he called me is because I had left a phone message asking him to, and the reason I had done that was because of what your mom had just told me." She went on to explain that the mom had told her that only a few weeks after the funeral this man had phoned her, saying that he had been present at Uncle Ted's death but couldn't seem to just get over it and move on. He had gone to the funeral at the church even though he was Jewish and knew no one there. "That was where," Miss Carol went on, "from the church bulletin, he had gotten the name of Robyn Rudgear as the closest adult relative. And then later he had phoned to ask if she would meet with him, because he wanted to know more about what was going on with Ted Costas in the last days of his life."

Miss Carol took a long sip of her tea. "Your mom turned him down, wouldn't meet with him."

"Big surprise," Joanie said.

"But for some reason she had kept his contact information. Yesterday, she volunteered to give to me. I think it was done for you, Joan — in appreciation that you can't just casually move on from his death either."

"But when he phoned, what did this man tell you!"

"Well, first of all, he said that back in late April he had invited your mom and anyone else in the family to the 'Ted Costas Memorial Game.' This was to be the last game of next year's spring training, and the same group of seniors from Baltimore who had gone down on the field after the game with Uncle Ted to run the bases planned to be there and re-experience that memorable moment. Then they planned to gather afterwards for a meal to process and share their memories of him and what that day had come to mean to them. Your mom turned down the offer."

"Again, big surprise. But can *we* go — will you take me to that game!"

"Wait up. There's new news, and it's good news for us. The Orioles have changed their spring training base to the other coast of Florida. So it won't be possible to return to that same Fort Lauderdale stadium and go down after the game and directly re-experience there what Manny — that's the doctor — described as your uncle's 'strange but wonderful death.'"

"What's the good news?"

"They're going to do it here in a month, and we're invited."

"Double wow. And who are these others?"

"A group of people from around here. Manny, a couple of older ladies, a man with his grandson, and one or two others knew each other casually and fell into the habit of staying at the same Fort Lauderdale hotel and sitting together at the same games each spring training. He's contacted all of them, and they all want to get together about this. After his death, they read the newspaper account of Uncle Ted's escape from the hospital and giving away his sleeper room to the mom with baby and paying for people's meals on the train, and they had personally seen him giving away the one hundred dollar bills at home plate after circling the bases, but they all have questions to ask. And, it seems, their own emotions to share. Of course, no running the bases now, but an evening together, with a shared meal."

Joanie was rocking back and forth in her chair, saying nothing, overwhelmed with the pictures in her head.

"What you've found of him from those boxes downstairs, and come to understand about him in your heart will mean much to them."

"Yeah. I really want to go, but it's scary too. Hearing them describe his dying there, having his heart attack on that field — I don't know."

Miss Carol smiled, touched her arm. "But it was a good death. And now there is something quite revealing. Manny said he'd heard your Uncle Ted utter words that sounded ecstatic as he was dying – some of the words hadn't been clear, so he had never been able to put it all together and make exact sense of, and yet what he'd heard – and the powerful, strange way that Mr. Ted said it – that continued to haunt him."

"What was the 'something quite revealing'?"

He told me that now the words have come together for him. He feels sure he knows exactly what Mr. Ted said in his last seconds on earth, and what he's made of it sounds totally right to me. You see, it seemed a major drawback to your uncle that he'd never had a father, except when he was quite young. And no grandfathers living that might have substituted after his dad died when he was six. It had made him feel rudderless, like in some deep down way he lacked guidance all his life. More than once he told me this. It became part of his religious hunger, his faith, as well."

"What were those words, Miss Carol – what were they?"

Joanie watched her face take on a gentle smile as she spoke them: "'Father never seen but in every deep yearning of my heart.'"

About The author

Menalcus Lankford has been a city planner
in Virginia and California, an English
professor for many years in Maryland, and
a lay Episcopal campus minister. In 2010 he
started the Dickens Society of Baltimore, and
in 2011 published a new interpretation of
Bleak House in *The Dickensian*.

www.ingramcontent.com/pod-product-compliance
Lightning Source LLC
Chambersburg PA
CBHW020729210626
46807CB00016B/508